The Pain of Silence

Alicia Bailey

To Toni

Best wishes

Alicia Bailey

Published in 2013 by FeedARead.com Publishing –
Arts Council funded

A CIP catalogue record for this title is available from the British Library.

Dedicated to my three children,
Melanie, Andrea and Nigel,
who never gave up in their persistence and
encouragement to write the story of Esther and Henry.

Acknowledgements

Thanks to the Royal Air Force Museum, London, especially Andrew Cormack FSA, for their supportive information about WRAFs during World War I. A special thank you to my daughter Andrea, without whom *The Pain of Silence* would have remained just that. Her editing and research skills carried me forward.

INTRODUCTION

The story you are about to read is based on a true story. The people, events and places all existed but several names and places have been changed to protect identities and some dates have been condensed.

When I left the Taylor's home for the last time in 1979 with the now infamous carrier bag, little did I realise that I would be writing their complex story some thirty or so years later. The Taylor's carrier bag has accompanied me to the Isle of Man, Cyprus and to several of my homes in Wales and England. Over the years, I have read and deciphered numerous letters, certificates, papers and photographs and put the puzzle of their mysterious lives together, painstakingly bit by bit.

Both Esther and Henry suppressed their emotions and kept secrets from everyone, including each other. They kept their untold stories as if in a tightly corked bottle, which for years ebbed and flowed with the tides of three continents. With each letter I read, I managed to ease a little more of the cork out, until finally the cork exploded releasing the truth, accomplishing something no one else was able to. Now I share with you their incredible lives.

I wished the Taylors could have known that every word written was with loving memories and great affection. I hope that wherever the Taylors are, Henry is playing his beloved music and Esther is continuing with her passion for growing beautiful flowers.

Alicia Bailey

"Most men lead lives of quiet desperation and go to the grave with the song still in them."

Henry David Thoreau

JANE

1971-1972

One

It was a warm day in May 1971 as I drove along with Sister Drew sitting at my side. I had mixed feelings about starting a new job at the age of forty-one. Would I like it? Would I be able to cope with all the situations arising from this new position as auxiliary nurse with the District Nursing Association? I convinced myself that any major crises arising would be dealt with by the nursing sisters. My job was just a question of using my limited training and common sense. All too soon, I learned that most emergencies could be resolved this way.

All these thoughts were whirling around in my head but my negative attitudes were quickly replaced by positive ones. I felt such pride in wearing our newly designed uniform. It was fashioned in style to blend with the District Nursing Sisters. A burgundy coloured tailored dress which had a small collar with a cream trim was offset by a burgundy pill box hat. We were also provided with a top coat and matching cardigan of the same colour to suit the different seasons. An essential part of our kit was a large bag which contained all the medical paraphernalia we needed for our patients. This dark blue bag completed the professional look. Eventually the auxiliary nurses in their burgundy uniforms would become a familiar sight in the town of Hemel Hempstead.

I suddenly became aware of the voice of Sister Drew.

"How many children have you Mrs Durrant? Where does your husband work?" She asked all the polite questions that one asks a new colleague on their first day. "What made you apply for the job?" That was a difficult one and I cannot recall now what my answer was.

During the course of the morning, I accompanied Sister Drew to the homes of all the patients who would be on my round. Although I was accepted and made welcome by them all, my nerves had taken a battering. I told myself that only I knew that I was a novice, whereas the patients thought I had years of experience. This did allay my worries a little, although Sister Drew still put the fear of God into me. I think she had her own struggle to contend with, as auxiliary nurses were a new idea within the district nursing service. Some senior colleagues saw it as a threat to the profession. However, auxiliary nurses on the district proved to be a valuable asset and took some of the pressure from these overworked nursing sisters.

My head reeled from all these thoughts, as I tried to recall all the instructions I had been taught.

I was not a happy nurse when I arrived at the last house of the morning. Forest Walk sounded a beautiful address but in reality it was a row of bungalows built without any imagination. A quick glance showed me that only one or two of the gardens were well tended. The others looked uncared for.

As Sister Drew rang the bell she said with a smile,

"You may find this lady a little distant at first," adding, "But you will be all right once she gets used to you."

A very thin tall man answered the door holding a large brown dog by its collar. His very first words to me were, "She won't hurt you." That comment related to the dog, of course. Dogs, I am never afraid of but the thought of meeting his wife made me nervous.

Sister introduced me. "This is Mrs Durrant." A frail old woman with unfriendly eyes looked upon me. She had a tightly closed mouth that looked like it would never smile. Just a nod of her head acknowledged my presence. My outstretched hand was ignored and I quickly placed it on the back of the chair I was standing behind.

I looked at Sister who seemed to have taken this attitude in her stride, as though this unwelcoming behaviour was the norm and not solely for my benefit.

A mighty bang forced the door of the sitting room open. The large dog bounded in followed by the tall thin man. He put his hand out to shake mine and introduced himself as Henry, Mrs Taylor's husband. I felt this was more acceptable and positive in comparison to his wife being so distant. I wasn't to speak to Henry again for a few weeks.

I thought to myself, a household that has such a loving dog like Tessa must have a more gentle side to it. When the time came to leave the house it was with great relief. "I will not need to accompany you next week. I can see you are quite capable." This was Sister Drew's parting shot to me.

Praise indeed from this experienced District Nurse who initially had made me feel very unsure of my own capabilities. I still felt a dread however, at the prospect of going solo the following week. It reminded me of when you take your driving test and pass. On your very next journey you realise that there is no one there to brake for you and forestall any mistakes.

Contrary to all my doubts and fears, the following week seemed to go well. It is true to say that during that week I constantly telephoned other nursing colleagues with problems that concerned me. On reflection, most of those calls were probably unnecessary. They were due to my lack of experience and confidence. I thought it was far better to seek advice from my more experienced colleagues, than to take chances with the patients' care.

Monday to Thursday passed by without any problems but the inevitable dreaded Friday arrived and with it my last patient of the week, Mrs Taylor. My car glided into the only vacant spot available in the bay opposite the bungalows. Why did I have to re-position it several times? I felt eyes were gazing at me. I had to tell myself to stop being paranoid. 'Be yourself' had always been my attitude to life. Why had that reasoning deserted me now? I walked reluctantly up the path towards the door. The smile on my face was false. Wonderful Tessa bounded towards me in recognition. Henry had the suspicion of a smile on his face in a silent greeting.

"Good morning and how are you today?" I asked.

The scowling face of Mrs Taylor glared at me.

"I don't know why they have to send somebody new. I am used to the other nurses. You will have to be careful with me as I have a bad heart. Didn't they tell you my heart is very weak?"

Mrs Taylor's fierce comments filled my mind with anxiety, so much so, I could feel my heart racing. Should I have collapsed, I didn't want her to give me the kiss of life. Alternatively, all that she would have to have done to bring me around, was to wave the glass of alcohol, that I had spotted on the mantelpiece, under my nose. The smell of brandy filled the modest sitting room. In seconds, I curtailed my thoughts as I realised that this was not a professional attitude.

Henry brought in the bowl of water I required. He didn't speak, only smiled when he gave it to me. Mrs Taylor must have instructed him to do this before my arrival, as I wasn't allowed to enter either the kitchen or the bathroom.

Trying to relate to Mrs Taylor I asked, "Do you have any children?"

"No," was said so vehemently that I realised I had made a huge blunder.

Whilst attending to her back I faced the sideboard which was pushed against a wall. I couldn't help but notice some photographs. On the wall facing me was a large picture of a boy who looked about nine or ten years of age. It was apparent to me that he was a child with special needs. The mirrored silver frame surrounding the photograph had seen better days and had the look of the swinging sixties about it. A second photograph, in a dark wooden frame, stood on the sideboard and was of a young man in Air Force uniform. I felt intrigued and imagined that there had to be a story behind these photographs, as Mrs Taylor had been adamant when she said they had no children. I felt sadness. Could this be what was wrong in this home?

My work was completed in silence. This met with Mrs Taylor's approval and seemed the way she preferred things to be. At this stage I knew that I would dread Fridays for as long as I had to care for her. Another thought occurred to me. Mrs Taylor seemed so cantankerous, what if she telephoned the Head Nursing Officer to have me replaced? There was nothing I could do other than wait and see.

"Goodbye, see you next week," were my final words to her. Henry had kept out of the way. Even when I called through the door a farewell greeting, there was just silence.

If my walk to the house was reluctant, the one back to the car was more so. I felt that I had been unable to connect with this patient. I had a two way conversation with myself on the way home. As long as I did my job well and to the best of my ability it would be fine. After all, I couldn't expect everyone to like me. If I couldn't make her warm to me then I would have to accept it.

Fridays came and went and still this patient remained withdrawn from me. Should I catch her unawares, looking at me, I would glimpse a different look in her eyes. It vanished as soon as our eyes met and the look of steel would return in an instant.

Six months or more passed. Each week Henry sauntered in and out with bowls of hot water or the towels I required. It was the depths of winter and on my next visit I noticed Henry sitting opposite his wife near the fire. I was waiting for him to vacate his chair but to my amazement he stayed sitting there, other than getting up to bring the things I required. This proved to be the pattern for the whole winter. It took a couple of weeks before Henry uttered a single word. Amazingly Mrs Taylor told me to call her Esther. She was still calling me Nurse but before too long, she started to call me Jane. At long last, I believed we were making some headway.

Spring soon followed and I got quite brave and started to involve Henry in an occasional remark. This was fine for a week or two but then the pitiable man was once again demoted to the kitchen. I tried to engage him in conversation on his trips to the living room with the toiletries but Esther resented it and made her feelings known. I realised that she was jealous and regarded me as one of her rights and not Henry's. This situation played on for some time but the poor man got bolder, as did I. We started to have little talks about the dog or snooker, things I knew he was interested in. Before too long Henry was back in the sitting room again and allowed to participate.

During this period of time I started to tell them about my family. One visit caught me by surprise because Esther asked after my children and enquired about what they wanted to do when they were adults. I couldn't believe that we had progressed that far. In fact, little did I know just how intertwined our lives would become.

I talked of my siblings, one of whom lived in Durban, South Africa but as soon as I mentioned this fact the whole atmosphere changed and we were back to square one and the cold war. What had I done? I couldn't imagine. They were still talking to me but the subject of my siblings or even mention of my mother became a 'no go zone.' I was completely floored as to the reason why. I tried to heal the rift so my next strategy was to ask them if they would like to visit my home."Would you like to come to lunch one day?"

"I don't know but we will think about it," was Esther's stern reply.

A couple of weeks passed by and out of the blue Henry enquired, "Is that offer of lunch still standing?"

I made a date for the following week so that there wasn't time for the invitation to be cancelled and it wasn't. I collected them as arranged and to my astonishment the lunch went brilliantly. This enabled Esther and Henry to meet my husband and son. Our relationship was now on the up again. If truth be told, they started to open up to me a little more. Esther told me that this was a second marriage for them both. The young boy whose picture hung on the wall above the sideboard was her handicapped son. The second picture was her other son. He had served in the Air Force but she couldn't bear to talk about him. I assumed he had been killed during the Second World War. My heart ached for them. Perhaps these tragic events accounted for their weird behaviour?

Over the next few months I learned a little more from Esther, always in whispers whilst Henry was out of the room or had popped to the local shops for some 'ciggies' or brandy. On one occasion, I was shown an unfinished shawl that Henry had knitted for their only baby. I thought I had finally made a break-through and gained Esther's trust. This was not so. The shawl was hastily wrapped up again in the fragile, aging tissue paper, secreted away and never mentioned again.

ESTHER
1899 - 1919

Two

I was born in 1899 in the beautiful county of Kent which was always called the Garden of England because of its abundance of orchards and hop gardens. The countryside around our house was beset with oast houses. The rotating cowls always intrigued me. I would stare up at them, longing for a gust of wind to propel them into a new position.

We moved to West Farleigh from Guildford when I was almost five years old. My childhood was a very happy one and I was much loved by my parents. My father adored me. In fact, my childhood would prove to be the most untroubled period of my life.

I was born on the cusp of a new century, during the last years of Queen Victoria's reign. My earliest recall of those idyllic days is at the age of three. Later in life, my father was able to confirm this when we had our wonderful talks. I was able to remember many things which surprised him. I recall my little feet treading on the cobbles which formed the path that twisted to match the contours of the garden. What a joy it was when I spotted the first snowdrops. I was so excited; their dainty little heads always seemed to dance in the breeze. Father once said they were really dancing. I was so young, everything I was told, I believed.

Our home was called Willow Cottage. A stone built cottage covered with Virginia creeper. It came complete with love, warmth and safety. The cottage had open fireplaces in all the rooms and when winter was at its coldest my father would light them all. To a child it was always cosy and welcoming. The stairs constantly creaked. Father tried everything he knew to remedy this. Beeswax was frequently packed into every stair tread but nothing succeeded.

Mother's kitchen table was scrubbed daily and was as white as her sheets. She would roll out pastry and chop garden vegetables on it. All manner of cakes and pies came into fruition on that wonderful table. When my sister Molly and I were little, Mother would lay the towels on its smooth surface to dry us off after being lifted out of the tin bath. At the end of a long tiring day, my parents would plonk themselves down at the table with a cup of tea and discuss the day's events and sometimes, things we were not meant to know about. Molly and I often heard them speak in hushed tones. If that table could have talked it would have revealed such secrets.

Father was always called Father. Even as an adult I couldn't hear or utter the word Father without feeling his presence, love and wisdom. Father was a gardener. He loved the whole of nature, combining gardening with his love for his fellow creatures. These qualities, I believed, to be the magic ingredients to life itself.

I can see him as though he were before me now. He wore old discarded trousers, a baggy jacket several sizes too big for him, both tied with string around his rotund middle. A battered black Homburg was always perched on his head and he insisted on wearing heavy duty walking boots, regardless of the weather. An old clay pipe never left his lips, even when the tobacco had long burned out. This image of him is eternally etched in my mind and engraved on my heart.

Father's labours in the garden gave such delight. It was never apparent to the eye that soil existed. Tall flowers such as hollyhocks, delphiniums, arum lilies and peonies graduated down to the smaller pinks, campanulas and primroses. Many more were interspersed between the fruit bushes which were my mother's domain, the whole garden creating a canvas of colour.

Molly, my sister, however, didn't share the same love. To her it was just a garden you played in. This was why I was allowed to pick the first snowdrops and Mother the first daffodils. What Molly did share was the excitement we felt, when we saw Mother come down the path with a large old blanket over her arm. We knew it meant we were going to have a picnic under the apple tree. We would jump up and down with excitement as though the occasion was a rare occurrence. In reality it happened frequently. Mother would return down the pathway with a heavy tray piled high with jams, butter and scones plus salad from the garden.

As children we thought everyone had the same blessing. Our larder had shelves filled with Mother's bottles of jam, pickled onions, and red cabbage. In fact, everything grown by Father. There were even dried flowers for the table. His gardening skills were used by many in the village and generated our income. The only exception was that of tending the church grounds. This Father did voluntarily all his working life and repeatedly told Molly and me, "It is my work for the Lord."

Father's skills were accomplished but Mother's were just as first-rate. She was a proficient homemaker and had this inborn skill to nurture her young. She bandaged cut legs, dosed us with cough medicine and the dreaded cod liver oil when needed, inspected our heads for nits, bathed and cuddled us. She was an expert in loving children. How fortunate we were. Our parents had met and married, and continued to love each other for their whole lives.

I don't remember much about my elementary school other than a huge world map on the wall with the British Empire coloured in pink. I do remember I found learning multiplication tables, spellings and historical dates easier than some of my friends. Eventually I was one of the few to gain a scholarship to a girls' high school.

When I left school at sixteen, I really didn't know what I wanted to do. I went to work in an office but I wasn't happy. Each day dragged by and seemed endless but what else could I do? Most girls worked as domestics, some in shops and offices, and others as nannies to young children.

It was 1918, towards the end of the First World War and everything was upside down. My girl friends in the office at work were all talking about the Women's Royal Air Force, WRAF for short. They had seen posters in various places in the town centre saying:

WOMEN!
The Royal
Air Force
needs your
help!

The poster went on to state:

There is fit work for every
FIT WOMAN

I was nearly nineteen and it fired my imagination. It all sounded so glamorous. At last I could be treated like an adult, make my own decisions and do what I wanted. We had to apply at the nearest Employment Exchange. The Post Office had been very helpful by supplying the address. We now had the perfect solution to our immediate futures. However, it was quite a performance to acquire the necessary papers in order to proceed.

The enrolment procedure was much more involved than any of us had expected. The selection process was very complex. You had to make decisions according to your skills. Stringent health examinations were carried out. Women from very under privileged backgrounds, especially those from polluted cities, often failed the medical. They were frequently found to be suffering from the complaints associated with living in such poor, harsh conditions. It saddened us to think that so many people were still living in such terrible housing.

The work of the WRAF was divided into four basic trades: Clerks and Store women, Household, Technical and Non-Technical. Women were allocated positions according to their skills, as initially, very little training was given. I was very fortunate as I was a clerk with the qualifications of a shorthand typist. At that time I hadn't realised that it meant I would be one of the highest paid. The women allocated to the Household section were paid the lowest wage even though they did back breaking work and worked the longest hours. The WRAFs released the men for more active service.

It was at this stage that I became conscious of the enormity of the task ahead. We were not enlisting for the glamour or the release from parental control. Our country really did need our help. I was now able to understand the need for a persuasive enrolment campaign. Fit women were desperately needed. One thing really annoyed me and made me angrier than I would have believed. The so called, upper class and well educated women were immediately enrolled as officers. How disgraceful that seemed to me. The rest of us, the hoi polloi, were known as Members.

I had to make another decision when I completed the Enrolment Form for Members. There were two categories called, 'Mobiles' and 'Immobiles'. Mobiles lived in quarters on or near their workplace, whereas Immobiles lived at home and were attached to their local station.

I decided to be an Immobile and live at home. I surmised I would probably be based at West Malling which was my nearest RAF Base. We had no worries with respect to transport as the RAF informed us that we Immobiles would be collected by a lorry or char-a-banc first thing in the morning and dropped off in the late afternoon.

Our Standing Orders were strict. The WRAF Constitution and Regulations were contained in a pocket size blue booklet, setting out the standard expected of us. Standing Orders was the name given to these sets of rules and one had to adhere to them. Behaviour was constantly monitored. We were not allowed to smoke on duty or in the street and our uniform had to be worn correctly. There would be no jaunty wearing of caps. I rather think whoever made that rule realised that women liked to wear their civilian hats differently. We knew what our best angle was. I had the notion that all these rules would impress my parents, especially Father who made all the big decisions in our home. I hoped the fact that I had applied to be an Immobile and would remain living at home would convince him of the virtues of becoming a WRAF.

After a couple of days my parents signed their consent and I was able to complete the forms, forward them to the Air Force and wait. Within a couple of weeks I received a letter to say I had been accepted providing the rigorous medical gave me a clean bill of health, which it did, fortunately. I could not believe it. I was now Member Esther Brownlow, a WRAF and very proud to be called so.

Eventually, my office friends and I were all accepted. It was very inspiring to be kitted out with so much uniform. I must admit the bloomers and lisle stocking were atrocious but I liked the light blue of our uniform. We were also issued with white cotton shirts to wear under our jackets. When starched, it made the collar of my jacket lie beautifully. It was well worth the effort and only took a few minutes to accomplish. I had three embroidered badges on the top of my right sleeve – WRAF, a capital *I* for Immobiles and the Air Force emblem. With hindsight I cannot say the uniforms did anything to present the female form in an attractive light. Mind you, I should imagine that could have been its purpose.

It was a new chapter in my life. Although we were recruited as office workers or writers, as some of us were known, basic drills still had to be learnt. We had to know how to march correctly, salute our officers, behave in the mess halls and how the officers were ranked. I found it all very exhilarating.

One part of our training surprised me. We were taught

how to deal with the enemy if we suspected that members of the public could be spies. When the first basic course was finished, I was back employed in the same capacity as my previous boring civilian job. My job description was that of a writer.

The shops were empty of fancy clothes, which saved us money so we could do a little saving but for what I didn't know. What an innocent I was. The few close friends I had made used to go out to the pictures or for long walks and I would tag along with them. We were a happy little band and I'm sorry to say we only thought of what we were doing, and not of the major happenings on the front. My excuse can only be that we were young and like the youth of today, self obsessed.

I cannot remember who told us, not that it mattered, but we learned that the troops based in Hyde Park were a Canadian Regiment. This sounded very alluring to all of us. Now, all we had to do was to decide how best to follow up the interest that we felt. A decision was made to go to London on the cheaper, earlier train at 6.30 a.m. Saving on the train fare enabled us to have enough funds to buy a hearty breakfast that would sustain us for the whole day. Clothes were not a problem to those of us who wore uniform.

We left the station aglow with anticipation and made our way to Hyde Park, not knowing exactly what we would do when we got there. Men in uniform were everywhere. Like us they were on leave, coming to look at London's historical buildings, monuments and places of interest, that had only been read about in books at school. It was fascinating and far too much to take in on our first visit. We made a pact to return, perhaps next time, staying overnight at the women's hostel, so that we could go to a dance in the evening.

We returned home very tired and yet exhilarated because we had been able to make our own decisions. For years our parents had made the rules for us, which is how it should be in the formative years but now we could make our own choices.

A couple of weeks passed before our next visit to London. It took quite a bit of organising to synchronise our leaves. This time, our excitement rose as our clothes were sorted. What one didn't have, the others did and so we helped each other out. One civilian outfit each was all that was needed to impress the boys on the Saturday night. Our choice of perfume was limited to rose or lavender, both of which were home made. We crushed lavender heads and pounded them, adding two spots of any oil (we used cooking oil).The same applied to the rose petals. Perfume was virtually unobtainable in the shops and had it been available, we certainly didn't have the money to buy it. Finally everything was organised and we couldn't wait for the weekend to come.

We stayed at a hostel which was clean although we didn't have the luxury of bedrooms, only dormitories, six beds in each. Once we had settled in we began our preparations for the evening ahead, we washed then set our hair before we applied our makeup and finally dressed. On completion of this female routine we told each other just how beautiful we looked. Youth carried us on winged feet to the forces' club.

As we approached the club the noise from the big band and the general hubbub of everyone enjoying themselves, drifted towards us on the chilling night air. As we neared the entrance the sound was deafening but at the same time, very exciting. We were surrounded by servicemen of all nationalities. We thought this had to be life at its best. How simple it appeared when we were young.

Several dances later I realised a young man was directing his smile at me, which I might add, I returned. However, he didn't ask me to dance and made no move to walk over.

All too soon it was time to go. We collected our trench coats hurrying for the exit whilst trying to put them on. We wanted to avoid the rush. Suddenly I was being helped with mine. It was the smiling soldier.

"Will you be coming next week?" he enquired.

"Who knows? We are WRAFs. It all depends on our leave."

Three weeks later we were back and so was he. We danced several dances that night and I realised that he was a Canadian. His accent was strong and the flash on his epaulette confirmed Canada. This fascinating man's name was Thomas James Barratt. He had fair hair with an even fairer complexion and attractive hazel eyes. He wasn't particularly tall but taller than me. However, at 5 feet 2 inches most people were. Thomas was a Sergeant serving with the 95th Battalion, part of the Canadian Overseas Expeditionary Force. During the interval he asked me to go outside so that he could kiss me.

I was very indignant. "I am not that sort of girl."

He smiled and said he was testing me. Had I done what he requested he wouldn't have been interested in me. I remember thinking; it's a man's world. Women are condemned if they do and condemned if they don't. When we finally parted company we promised to stay in contact.

Weeks went by, letters passed between us. I discovered Thomas was seven years older than me. He told me he was from a place called Belleville, in Ontario. He had a family - a mother, father, brother and two sisters. He wrote such romantic letters. I was in love. My next visit to London to meet him was by myself. I stayed the night at the same hostel. We spent the day strolling around London arm in arm. At the end of the day I found it incredibly hard to say good bye and return to Kent.

It was such a whirlwind romance. We became engaged with the blessings of my parents. My father told me years later that his and my mother's hearts had sunk with the news. They realised that I plus any family I might have in the future, would be thousands of miles away in a country unknown to both of them.

The wedding plans went ahead. Little did we realise how hard the governments of each country had made it for marriages to take place. Brides were vetted and counselled in order to make them aware of how big a step it was to take.

Thankfully, all went well with my interview and preparations for our wedding proceeded. It was 1918 and I was nineteen years old.

Three

Several months later, with the Congregational Church in Guildford booked, it was full steam ahead. I informed my parents that I wished to be married in the church where I had been christened. We knew from the start that Thomas's family would not be able to attend. Great debates took place and we concluded that only my closest family would be present. It would not only save us money but also show Thomas that we were well aware that he would be missing his family.

Fellow servicemen and women from Thomas's regiment and my squadron filled the pews and added to the volume of sound, nearly raising the roof during the singing of the hymns. They were so supportive. Thomas's commanding officer attended, which was a complete surprise and uplifting for him. The reception was held at Willow Cottage. Somehow, Mother had managed to acquire the ingredients for the wedding cake with everybody in the village helping out. It seemed that Thomas, being a Canadian added some prestige to the occasion. I could not think why. Honeymoons were unheard of, so, like many other couples, we only managed a few days away together, staying in a small guest house by the sea at Cliftonville.

During the first world war the shortage of food got progressively worse as more and more ships that were transporting food were torpedoed. The situation became dire. After roughly two years at war Britain had just six weeks' worth of food left and therefore had to start food rationing at the end of 1917.

My father's skills guaranteed that we always had vegetables, eggs, and fruit. Mother bartered with neighbours and whoever had an abundance of crops would share. Some had nothing spare but offered to take in laundry or care for the children. The war brought out the best in some people. Class distinction was placed on hold to some extent, sadly to return as soon as hostilities ended.

Hundreds of thousands of men returned from the war, their lives shattered, never to be the same again; suffering from the effects of gas, trench fever and amputated limbs. Many were blinded or suffering from shell shock. It was not a time of joy for any young couple facing their future. Married life was difficult with us both being serving members of the armed forces. Thomas was still based at Hyde Park. We spent quite a lot of time apart as we had to adhere to the many regulations and formalities laid down by both the Canadian Army and the Women's Royal Air Force.

In the months that led up to the 11 November Armistice of 1918, armies and navies from all over the world had begun to disperse. Thomas was called before his commanding officer and told that the embarkation for the return of his regiment to Canada was imminent. The authorities would try to accommodate service men with British wives on the same ship. However, with the shortage of shipping, a war bride might be placed on any ship that had space available. This news alarmed us greatly. I would have to seek advice from my superiors. To my relief, the powers that be were well prepared for this and appropriate forms were produced within a few days. The perusal of these forms made me aware of what a serious step I was about to take.

I was quite fearful of the unknown. My love for Thomas was steadfast but my acceptance by his family was of great concern to me. We were going to have to live with them until we managed to obtain a house of our own but we couldn't strive for that until Thomas found a job.

Britain was in a deplorable situation. The war had been a catastrophe. Nearly three quarters of a million British men were estimated to have died and more than a million and a half had been severely wounded during the conflict.Thousands of returning servicemen were without jobs, many were hungry; some were even going without food, only surviving on what they could beg or steal. Having nothing meant just that and some families fell apart under this terrible pressure.

Winter had arrived and with it a virulent virus known

as the Spanish Flu. Most doctors and the majority of nurses were still at the front treating war casualties. Those who succumbed to the virus took second priority to the thousands of injured and shell shocked men who occupied hospital beds. Ultimately the virus killed five times more people than the war.

With all this in my mind my anxiety for my future life never left me. I realised only too well that similar conditions were being felt by the Canadians or any country with returning servicemen. I tried to hide all these fears and apply myself to the tasks ahead, if only to reassure the people who surrounded me with their love and protection. It was very difficult.

A cloud descended on Willow Cottage. I wandered around the garden. Every leaf and flower appeared to droop as though they sensed the sorrow of my impending departure. Even the dew that clung to the leaves seemed to take its time to say goodbye. Yet, everything else looked so normal and beautiful on that winter morning. It seemed no different from when I was a child. Why do things have to change? I think that was the moment I realised that I was an adult and life would never be the same again.

It took me several weeks to sort through the clothes from my wardrobe as they had to be suitable for the harsh winters of Ontario. Thomas's family had advised me well. Our luggage allowance was one case each, plus one for a couple, making three in all. It seemed such a small amount of space to put in a life time of memories and essential winter clothing.

Packing made all the feelings of apprehension return tenfold. It was truly happening. I was a soldier's wife and I was going to live in a vast new country and live with strangers. How I wished Father could come with me and settle me in. He could always make things right for everybody.

Days were marked off on the calendar. Silence and heavy hearts weighed down the household with sporadic tears flowing from us all. An assortment of farewells had to be endured. I felt a mixture of excitement, at the venture that lay ahead, also nervous and contemplative about the life changing decision I had made.

Departure day arrived and it was now time to leave. Saying goodbye to Mother and Father was unbearable as I really didn't know when I would see them again. I had never seen my parents cry. I felt so guilty witnessing their tears.

Thomas and I sat in silence for most of the train journey to Southampton, each of us with our own thoughts. Thomas was to tell me later that his heart was full of pain for me, also remorse because he was over-joyed to be sailing to his own country and delighted at the prospect of seeing his family again whilst I was leaving mine behind.

Thomas had changed. The young carefree man that had left Canada now had the responsibility of a young wife who was scared about the unknown and needed protecting. Whilst in England he had met many new people who had influenced him in several ways. We can all learn from other people's experiences in life. Thomas knew only too well, that had the war not ended when it did, he would now be in the trenches fighting the Germans. He realised that his life could have had a very different ending and that he shouldn't waste a moment in negative thinking.

Our arrival at Southampton seemed to revive, yet again, all the trepidation I had felt. Having Thomas at my side gave me more confidence but nothing relieved my low spirits. We were surrounded by masses of people all rushing in the same direction, some in uniform, others like ourselves were in civvies. As I shuffled along in the throng I started to look at all the many faces and tried to pair them up. I was always doing this and usually found that I mismatched folk. I would have been useless as a marriage broker. I was somewhat surprised to see so many children. My perception was that the Canadian troops had done their best to increase the world's population!

At last the queue to embark was on the move and we thought that another hour would see us in our cabin. We could hear voices raised in protest. It sounded as though it was coming from the front of the line.

All too soon we discovered the reason why so many people seemed upset and we shared their dismay. It was announced that married couples were not allowed to travel together and they were to be separated on different decks. Some passengers were demanding to be allowed off so they could wait for another boat. An official explained to those of us that could hear above all the clamour, that should anyone choose to disembark, it could be a further year before being offered another passage. He informed us that there were several thousand Canadian soldiers and their dependents awaiting transportation to Canada. He finally shouted at the top of his voice, "There are not enough ships decommissioned to transport this volume of people."

Silence fell on the crowd. We hadn't appreciated that we were in fact the fortunate ones. By the end of the war Canadian soldiers were marrying British and European women at the rate of 300 a week. The magnitude of the problem must have been a logistical nightmare to the Canadian authorities.

I loathed sharing with complete strangers but every available space was allocated. Extra bunks were added to most of the cabins; so many, that some doors were unable to close properly. I felt sorry for the pregnant women. There was no privacy and modesty went by the board. The system was in place for a reason and we had to abide by the rules laid down.

The first morning I managed to find Thomas and we grabbed some breakfast together. We both felt very close to tears. We didn't realise it at the time but it proved to be the only official occasion that we ate together in the mess. Subsequently, we decided we would each take something extra from the mess hall and share it on deck at our chosen rendezvous point. Luckily, there was always plenty of food for everybody.

We became very adept at breaking the rules, as had we kept to them we wouldn't have seen each other until we disembarked. We managed to meet often and we became quite good at beating the system. That was never to be repeated during our lives. Somehow, the system always seemed to win.

Two women from my cabin came from London, two from Kent, which included me of course, with the last pair coming from Yorkshire. The women came from all over Britain, due to the Canadian troops being posted everywhere.

Sea sickness was rife and I felt dreadful. I dragged myself out of the cabin, tried to keep warm and within reach of the lavatory. It was exhausting and I felt at the time, that dying might be preferable. Later, I was ashamed of my thoughts when I discovered that so many people on board were seriously ill.

A rumour circulated among the passengers that a few people had died, but we felt that, that was all it was, a rumour. Sadly we heard afterwards that it was the harsh and terrible truth. Influenza had taken its toll. The captain ordered parts of the ship to be isolated. That was an added worry for those of us whose husbands were in those areas. It was sobering to think that those unfortunate people, who had died, boarded the ship with the same dreams as us. Fate plays some cruel tricks.

Days passed by, we dreaded each one, for fear of the virus spreading. Thankfully, Thomas managed to pass a message to me via a member of the crew, telling me that all was well with him.

We met up on the morning of our arrival in Canada, afraid to let each other go. How thankful we were and how lucky to have survived, when others had not been so fortunate. We had arrived safely and now our future beckoned to us.

Noise abounded everywhere. Towering cranes loomed in the sky, swinging their rope cradles aloft, whilst crew members shouted commands to the stevedores lining the quay, waiting to off load cargo. The intense cold took our breath away making us realise that what had served us as winter coats in England, were totally inadequate for the harsh Canadian winter.

Thomas took off his coat and placed it around my shoulders. Within seconds he was shivering more than I was. We breathed in icy air which returned as hot steam. I suddenly panicked, sickness welled up from the pit of my stomach and I pleaded with Thomas to ask the Captain if we could stay aboard for the ships return to England.

He shook his head disconsolately. I knew it was an impossible request but I was at my lowest ebb. Thomas looked devastated at having to deny me my wish and I think he realised for the first time that he would have to make decisions for both of us. I summoned an inner strength from somewhere and hugged my shivering husband. I told him that we would be all right and that it was just my nerves getting the better of me. It was our future and we would go forward and meet it together. I could see and feel relief uplifting his whole body, conveying his strength and determination to me. I was comforted, our spirits were as one.

Army officials appeared, complete with clipboards, lists and large megaphones. We were herded into groups according to the different states we were bound for. We were given written instructions, train and identity cards, plus food boxes sufficient for the journey. Everything was carried out with the usual competence one came to expect from the armed forces.

Gradually smiles and relaxed faces appeared as everyone realised they were one step nearer to home. We all went to various numbered trains in high spirits. Thomas and I quickly found our carriage with its numbered seat. It was wonderful to feel the train's warmth. As we settled ourselves down, we decided that as we were very hungry we would start on one of our food boxes. Whilst we consumed the delicious contents we introduced ourselves to our fellow travellers. All our troubles were temporarily pushed to the far recesses of our minds whilst we dealt with the immediate situation. Convincing words of encouragement were uttered by us all. Looking back, I realise now that we were shoring each other up and using one another for support.

I would have so much to tell Father and Mother in my first letter. I asked Thomas, "Do we have enough Canadian currency to buy a stamp?" We looked at each other and started to laugh. In seconds the whole carriage had erupted with laughter. Somehow the laughter turned into a singsong. It was uplifting and our spirits rose. My first day in Canada was truly memorable.

The journey seemed to go on forever. We delayed consuming our second food box. Thomas didn't remark on the distance just how wonderful the countryside looked. Snow covered the pines making them look mysterious and at the same time forbidding, scenes that I had only seen in books or films. Occasionally we spotted animals which Thomas named. They all looked like deer to me. Stations came and went with such speed that trying to decipher their names was almost impossible. I managed to catch the names of some; one was Fallowfield and another Napanee. How wonderful they sounded. In the years that followed I managed to acquaint myself with most of their names.

Tired heads fell on to adjacent shoulders, a few snores plus mutterings filled the carriage. Somehow we felt these people, who were previously strangers, were now our close friends, bonds which in other circumstances might not exist.

ELIZABETH BARRATT
1919

Four

After a disturbed night's sleep I awoke abruptly in the early hours of the morning. It wasn't from the brightness of the full moon gleaming through the crack in the curtains; it was more to do with me dwelling on the events of the past year. So much had happened to us.

Our eldest son Thomas had left Victoria College to enlist in the Canadian Army which was attached to the British Army. I was very anxious about whether he had made the right decision or not. His father was also concerned.

I decided to voice my unease over the breakfast table. I asked, "Son, your father and I are worried for you. Why put your life at risk when it is avoidable? You don't have to enlist."

Thomas was adamant, "If our ancestors, on both sides of the family, hadn't sailed dangerous seas in over-crowded boats to a new life, we wouldn't be living here in Canada now."

I was stumped, as to how, to give an answer. Thomas was right and what he said was true. We were just thankful our other son, Wilfred, was too young to enlist.

Thomas sailed for England in 1917 and it wasn't too long before we received out first letter postmarked London. He was based at Marble Arch in Hyde Park. We couldn't imagine what that must have looked like to the British, their royal park festooned with enormous tents. According to Thomas, it was a canvas city consisting of large field kitchens, medical facilities plus all the living quarters.

Thomas wrote of the hardships facing the British people. Food rationing was in force, all chocolates and candy had disappeared. Thomas said it was impossible to find a store where you could make a purchase of choice. You had to have what the store had left in stock or nothing. We felt sadness for the Brits.

In his next letter Thomas spoke of a large balloon that had floated over London. It was called a Zeppelin, a German airship. He told us of that Londoners had flooded on to the streets and looked skywards in fear and horror. The word 'gas' had quickly spread amongst the growing crowd. On this occasion the Zeppelin was on a reconnaissance mission and had little impact other than a psychological one. However, it created mayhem.

We felt Thomas's letters always related something which conveyed sadness. He was expecting to join the action in France or Belgium but the easier life he was experiencing in England frustrated him. This was not so for us. As anxious parents we were nothing but relieved.

Quite suddenly the letters changed in their content. He

had met a girl at a dance. She was a WRAF serving in the British Air Force. Her name was Esther and she was a very nice girl. We were pleased to hear some cheering news but were a little concerned about the friendship. Should it develop in to something more, we could find that our son would want to remain in the UK.

More letters followed, each one more animated than the last. It became clear to us that Thomas and Esther loved each other. His brother and sisters, like us, had mixed emotions about the news. The family all shared the same concern. Eventually, Thomas told us of their plans to marry. They both sounded so happy. Esther's father wrote a beautiful letter to us, assuring us that they were very much in love. However, Esther's parents shared the same uneasiness as us. Esther was still so young at nineteen and both families shared the worry about where they would live. Would they settle permanently in England or would Thomas bring his bride to Canada?

It saddened us that we would not be able to attend the wedding in Guildford. Instead we had a reception here in Belleville, timed to synchronise with their actual ceremony. We toasted the happy couple and wished them many happy years together. It was a day of laughter and joy inter mixed with tears.

The end of the war in 1918 meant the end of so many young soldiers dying on the front but thousands would be returning to civilian life in Canada alongside Thomas and Esther. I wondered what future lay ahead for them all.

Esther wrote several letters to us. She had a way with

words. Every letter endeared her to our family. It was wonderfully uplifting to read that the newlyweds were intending to live in Ontario.

The day of Thomas and Esther's demobilisation was fast approaching. The entire family helped spring clean every nook and cranny of our house and garden and preparations were made for a 'Welcome Home' party. Our youngest daughter doubled up with her older sister, vacating her bedroom for her big brother and his new bride.

We all walked around the house with permanent grins on our faces. All we needed now was the estimated time of arrival at Montreal. We were beside ourselves with anticipation. My new daughter-in-law had won me over with her delightful letters. Esther and I were both certain that we would get along well and hopefully form a close relationship. It was a good place to start.

ESTHER

1919 - 1940

Five

"Esther, Esther."

It was Thomas waking me up. I was dreaming that Thomas was calling me in from the garden at Willow Cottage."We are here. Wake up sleepyhead," he shouted.

I couldn't believe it. All my planning to be smart and presentable went out of the window. I brushed my newly bought, very chic hat, dusted down my coat and Thomas rubbed our shoes with a crumpled up piece of newspaper. This was executed with great haste as we wished to look our best when we arrived.

The train came to a gradual stop. Fellow travellers got up and shook hands with one another, others gave warm embraces and some people were crying. We were breaking a bond that had been formed. Good wishes were passed on to those passengers remaining on the train who were travelling further to their destination.

When we gazed out of the window, it seemed as though the whole town had turned out to greet us. A military band was playing and Union Jacks flirted with the Red Ensign as they flew side by side. Suddenly

Thomas started yelling because he had spotted his family on the fringe of the vast crowd. We were in Belleville at long last.

An immediate feeling of panic overrode the excitement I felt. I had grown up in such a loving and protected environment but now I felt daunted and unprepared. All at once Father's presence seemed to be there with me, supporting me, giving me that extra strength I so badly needed.

Broad welcoming smiles were on everyone's faces as we pushed our way through the masses. This large crowd of people couldn't be here to greet us, surely, but they were. I soon realised Thomas's relatives were as apprehensive as I was. I wondered how they would react to me. The whole family, especially Thomas's mother, did all they could to dispel my nerves. They asked lots of questions and made me smile when they teased Thomas. It was the start of me being a member of the Barratt family. Acceptance was all I needed.

Father's wise guidance had once again supported me, showing me that each and every one of us has to face fear and uncertainties in our lives. He had taught me that love is the bedrock of life but even with this knowledge, I knew that my future path might not always be as smooth.

Finally we arrived at the Barratt house. Four large paved steps swept up in a curve to the front porch where a huge banner with, 'Welcome Home Esther and Thomas,' hung from the red brick arch. We made our way through the front door and discovered folk everywhere. The

Barratts had generously invited neighbours and friends to the party. The house was heaving with people.

Tables were laden with amazing food of every kind. One table was covered with a beautiful lace cloth starched to perfection. There were plates of cucumber, egg and ham sandwiches, home baked bread and buttered scones with jams and cream. This was complimented by a fine bone china tea service. Tiny Union Jacks were fastened to the sides of the cloth and larger versions were draped from each end of the mantelpiece. My new family had worked extremely hard to make me feel at home. We were totally overcome by this loving display of welcome but also exhausted from our journey. I found it hard to hold back my tears as Thomas hugged me.

Later that night we climbed the stairs to our tiny bedroom and quickly fell asleep, utterly exhausted, taking with us the glory of the day. Tomorrow a new life would begin for us both.

Next morning I awoke with a start. The Barratt family were up and about, creating lots of commotion as they got their breakfast. I lay in bed gazing up at the ceiling and pondered on the enormity of what I had done. Shortly afterwards Thomas woke up. Our faces were so close, that as we stared into each other's eyes, I wondered if he could read my thoughts.

We spent our first morning discussing our future with Thomas's parents. They gave us valuable advice; after all, they knew only too well what the current employment situation was. Hundreds of men had returned from the war and all would be seeking work. Some would have the added worry of providing for a wife, whilst others would have returned with children as well.

We listened carefully to Thomas's parents as they advised us. They asked questions that we hadn't even asked ourselves, such as what Thomas wanted to do with respect to his future or indeed, what had he qualified to do whilst being in the army. Before joining up he had been a student at Victoria College in Toronto. In some ways it sounded discouraging but at the same time it was very honest. One good piece of advice was, for us to take two or three days off before looking for work, so that Thomas could familiarise me with the town. This would give me a chance to get to know my way around.

Belleville was situated on the mouth of the Moira River in the Bay of Quinte and had a population of around 12,000 and prior to the war it had been a thriving town.

Thomas started my tour of the town by taking me to Victoria Park which was right on the water front. It was spectacular to see so many sailing boats and I could easily imagine myself visiting there frequently. It was fascinating as there was so much to watch. We then left the park, walked along Front Street and headed towards City Hall which was built in 1873 and was Gothic in style. The building was built entirely out of brick and had a tower which stood 185 feet high; making it one of Belleville's better known landmarks. Each side of the tower had a clock face so we had no excuse for not realising the time. Next, we made a quick u-turn into

Pinnacle Street, hastily walking past the Hotel Quinte before going off to explore some shops.

We attempted to visit as many as possible before exhaustion slowed us down. We compared them with the shops in England and decided some were better, as they appeared to carry more stock. We both noticed that many shops had a section in their window displaying available jobs. We made up our minds to return within the next few days to see what was on offer.

The following morning we ate breakfast at a leisurely pace then decided to return to the shops to read the job advertisements we had noticed the day before. We each took a column and read them out aloud if we thought the vacancy was suitable for Thomas. However, all our enthusiasm waned steadily as nothing seemed appropriate. If you did have a particular skill and were a returning serviceman you were given priority so although it wasn't to be that day, we felt it wouldn't be too long before Thomas would find something suitable.

All too soon the dream was shattered. Virtually all the applicants were returning servicemen so the applications were by the dozens if not hundreds. Some of the Canadians were anti war brides and I couldn't understand their attitude. We were lonely, missing our parents as well as short of money. Fortunately, I was able to shrug off their animosity as so many more peoples' kindness outweighed their snide remarks.

Weeks turned into months and Thomas became despondent at not be able to find a job. Our savings were diminishing at a fast rate. Everything was made worse as I couldn't get a permit to work and we had counted on my office skills to boost our income.

Our tiny cupboard of a bedroom that used to be our little haven began to feel like a prison. We waited until we went out for a walk to discuss things that worried us. Even our sex life was put on hold, which resulted in such tension between us. I knew we had to persevere and be patient. It was only the belief that there would be a job for Thomas sometime soon, that kept us going.

My instinct proved right. A friend of Thomas's put his name forward to a local magistrate when the post of Clerk to the Court had become vacant.

Thomas was recommended to apply. Having lived in England served him well, for this experience gave him an advantage over several other applicants. I'm still uncertain as to why but it seemed having an English wife was also considered a bonus.

Thomas finally had a job and we had something to celebrate. We could now make definite plans for our future. Thomas was to be based at the Court House in Pinnacle Street, which was one of the roads I had explored in Belleville when we first arrived.

With Thomas working we could now afford to pay rent. I was given the job of finding somewhere to live. It took me a month before I found a suitable apartment within an old large house. We happily paid a month's rent for the deposit.

We were able to move quite quickly as it came

furnished. The flat had a large living room, same sized bedroom plus a small fitted kitchen. We were fortunate to have our own lavatory. This was luxury indeed as we had to share the bathroom. Each flat had a designated day for bathing and doing the weekly wash. Most of the house was warm in the winter which made the drying of the laundry comparatively easy. I was so thrilled to see a brass plate with the words, *'Mr & Mrs Thomas Barratt,'* screwed onto a wooden panel to the left of the front door.

During the move we learned that on our arrival at the Barratt home, Alice, one of Thomas's sisters had moved out of her little bedroom for us. She hadn't let on and not a word of complaint had been uttered by her.

Mom and Pop Barratt had provided us with a home and had kept us in food since our arrival. We were thankful for their support at the start of our married life. Now we would be able to begin our lives together in our new home.

Six

We quickly settled down to married life, appreciating our own space and privacy. Each day seemed better than the last. I was pleased to keep our little apartment in pristine order. I made a housework rota which I was forever changing as I discovered more about running a home. Meals were planned with Thomas's favourites to the fore.

My only anxiety was awaiting my next mail from England. Father was the letter writer. I needed to know that all was well with the family as I had sent two letters already, telling them about our move to the apartment. It was so important for my parents to know that we had our own home and that Thomas had a good job, making sufficient money to support us. Both Mother and Father needed to hear news that would gladden their hearts, taking away any anxieties that they might have had. It took between two to three weeks for letters to arrive from England. I was impatient.

Finally, the much longed for letter from my father

arrived. My hands were trembling so much I had to be careful opening it. I was immediately transported back to Willow Cottage. A little envelope was enclosed and inside it was a pressed snowdrop. My wonderful father had sent a piece of England to comfort me. I shed tears of gratitude for all the love I had received over the years, realising for the first time, that this was a gift and not a right. One little snowdrop had encapsulated the essence of my family's life and love. Soon our letters started to arrive in a regular pattern. We knew that answers from either side of the Atlantic would take their time coming. I was at peace knowing that all was well with both families.

Life continued with its established routine. It was a habit of mine to stop for a coffee whilst doing my household shopping. It was always at the same little cafe I had discovered in a back street. I loved going there because of its clientele and I would eaves drop on the conversations at the tables around me. They were so interesting with talk of politics and of the unemployment of returning servicemen. I found it all stimulating. It reminded me of similar tea shops in England. Customers here in Canada would discuss the same subjects as I'd heard at home. I concluded that people were much the same the world over when talking over a cup of tea or coffee.

On one such visit I was taken aback as I watched the cafe owner amble towards me with a broad smile on his face. He asked if he could join me at my table then promptly sat down and asked me if I would like a job. I wasn't even looking for a job and one found me. Thomas came home that night to a radiant wife with wonderful news. He was elated and by the end of the evening my lovely husband had almost spent the, as yet unearned, salary. He ignored the fact that I still had to obtain a work permit.

"We will start saving and have boxes for this and boxes for that but the most important box will be the Fare to England Box."

We hugged each other and kissed. Once more, my dear husband had thought of my needs first.

Christmas was fast approaching but I couldn't get into the spirit of it. Mom and Pop Barratt invited the whole family to share this special time at their house. Everybody tried to help me through this unsettled period. Father's first letter was dated 7th October and it was hard for me to accept that leaving home hadn't been the eternity it felt. So much had been accomplished in the past few months and yet homesickness filled my very soul.

On reminiscing I became conscious that now would have been the time of year that Father, Mother, Molly and I would go out to pick holly. We always knew where to look. Mistletoe was the hardest plant to find. On returning home we would be thrilled with our treasures. Father would pick the holly from the highest point of the tree so that Mother wouldn't prick her fingers quite so frequently when making the yuletide wreaths. As a countryman he knew that the higher holly grows the less prickly it is. The prickles are always longer at the bottom of the bush to protect the plant from grazing animals. My mother always made wreaths as a gift for our neighbours.

Wood was readily available to my father all year round. How we enjoyed wonderful fires particularly with apple logs burning, as they gave off a heady scent. It was little wonder that this particular Christmas, away from home, gave me a heavy heart. I told myself that I had to present a brave face to the world as my new family were doing their very best to make sure I enjoyed their Christmas festivities.

New Year's Eve was a time of reflection for everybody. Many had lost precious sons, husbands and brothers in the fighting. When the New Year greetings were exchanged, prayers of thanks were said for having survived the war, coupled with the comment that there must never be another one.

I was led to believe that Belleville had four distinct seasons with summer and winter weather being moderated by the Bay of Quinte and the near location of Lake Ontario. I recall we had average temperatures of -5°C but it dropped to below -19° C during my first winter. I had never seen so much snow in my life. In England we would have shivered and put more clothing on and raced to get to the chair closest to the fire. This was not so in Canada. They tackled the cold and snow in a different way. Most of the houses were well insulated and kept warm. On going out people would put on extra layers of clothing and upon their return they would simply removed the heavy outdoor layer. This way they did not need to have a vast wardrobe of winter clothing. As the Barratt's home was so warm and cosy no one needed to seize the warmest seat nearest the fire.

I had exciting news to share in my letters home as Thomas had taught me to ice skate. For weeks we had been watching and observing people having a wonderful time. I was scared but was persuaded by Thomas that ice skating was very simple to accomplish. It took an hour for me to progress enough to take both hands off the rail. Thomas proved to be very skilled but had kept it a secret to surprise me. Before long Thomas was skating backwards holding both my hands. I loved it and it was over three hours before we finally left the rink. On going to bed that night it dawned on me that I hadn't thought of England and home for the whole time we were on the ice. From that day onwards I begged Thomas to take me skating whenever we were free. He didn't complain once because he realised that the bubbly smiling girl he had married was back again. It was obviously the right medicine for me.

Thomas loved his job but he knew promotion wasn't possible without a degree in law. He continued to do his best and was considered a first class clerk by all the magistrates. My job at the cafe was obviously limited. I couldn't progress but I was happy enough enjoying the banter with the customers. It remained rewarding and I had the added bonus of working for a very kind boss. It was all that I needed. Although my wages were low, the amount when added to Thomas's salary kept us solvent.

Letters continued to fly back and forth between England and Canada. I wrote all the letters but Thomas always insisted on making a contribution - that of a row of kisses each time. Mother rarely wrote and I didn't mind because I knew it was a chore she hated. On the rare occasions that I had been away from home it was Father who had put pen to paper as he loved writing letters. He always said that he talked to the paper as he penned the words. It may sound ridiculous but when I read his letters I could hear his voice.

As our way of life became more established, time seemed to fly by. Both our jobs were stable and having a slight increase in our salaries had helped as the cost of living steadily rose. Mom and Pop Barratt continued to be the same loving and supportive parents. By now, Thomas's sister Patricia, had married and moved to Edmonton, Alberta which was over eighteen hundred miles away from all the family.

One evening Thomas came home from work looking very worried. The head magistrate had informed him that he wished to see him the next day. My poor husband was in such a state of unease. It didn't help that everyone knew that if the boss wanted to see you, you were in trouble. We didn't sleep well that night as anxiety infiltrated every thought that we had. We wondered what it could be about but everything was supposition and conjecture. On kissing him goodbye the next morning, I could feel him trembling. Visions of unemployment loomed large before us both.

It was a long day with each hour seeming to double in length. At long last I saw Thomas coming down the path, but his fedora prevented me from seeing his face. I couldn't wait for him to put his key in the lock and I threw the door open. Thomas's face was a picture of misery.

"What happened, what happened?" I asked over and over again.

"Sit down. Let's have a cup of tea first," he calmly said.

Astonished, I bellowed out, "What?"

He had been joking and on seeing tears flowing down my face he was contrite.

"Sorry, sorry. I was only teasing," he said, before he sat me down and let the story unfold.

On being called into the boss's office Thomas was nearly in a state of collapse which the astute magistrate quickly recognised. He told him swiftly that it was good news and invited Thomas to join him for a coffee. Thomas still couldn't guess what on earth this could be about.

A new government department had been formed called The Ministry of Food. It was set up to implement the 1920 Food and Drugs Act. Its task was not only to monitor all foods imported and exported but also to govern food production in Canada. All foods had to be passed fit for human consumption and had to be stamped when approved. The head magistrate had kindly recommended

Thomas for a senior post with this department. The court had furnished an excellent reference stating his skills and a copy was given to him. It said that he was intelligent, always carried out anything that was required of him; he had a great sense of responsibility and so much more. It ended with the magistrates expressing how much they would miss him but that he deserved to be able to further his career and that they had greatly appreciated his loyalty to them. What a reference from such esteemed members of society. We were ecstatic. Thomas's salary and pension rights would be considerably more than his present post. All he had to do now was pass the interview.

That day arrived. His suit was pressed and his shoes were so highly polished that you could see your face in them. All this attention to detail would help to give a good impression. A smiling Thomas left the house returning two hours later with the same smile on his face.

"I've got the job."

We sat grinning at each other all evening. Mom and Pop Barratt were promptly told and I wrote to my family immediately. We wanted everyone to share our happiness.

Everything changed for the better and with our increased income we were able to rethink our future. Thomas passed his trial period with flying colours so now we could relax and mull over our future plans. Our new finances enabled us to consider moving out of the apartment and into a house of our own. It was a happy time. Thomas was now able to take out a mortgage and as soon as I finished my day's work I would march into the house agents and set about viewing properties. Eventually I found our dream house. It was everything we wanted. It was a detached brick built house in a pleasant road in Belleville. Steps led up to the covered veranda that ran along the entire width of the property. The bricks were a warm orange and under the eaves were exquisite interlocking terracotta tiles. There were plenty of windows including one at each end of the attic. It had four large bedrooms, a massive sitting room, a huge kitchen plus a very nice garden. I couldn't wait for Thomas to see it for himself. I felt the house very much befitted an Inspector from the Ministry of Food. When he did view the property, the only word he said was, "Perfect."

Thomas's remark filled me with delight. I could not believe that we were going to buy the house and become an established family who might live here all our lives, hopefully bringing up any children we might have. Four bedrooms were really advantageous, as now we could have visitors to stay. I promised myself that I would be the best wife possible. Life was proving to be good to me. My new country and new family had made me feel so welcome. I felt truly blessed.

There were lawyers to instruct, a mortgage to be arranged and papers to sign. Everything was happening all at once. One of my missions was to furnish our new home. My instruction from Thomas was, "Only buy the essentials, no luxuries."

Moving day came and every Barratt was on hand to give us help. Laughter, jokes and cups of tea and coffee made the work a pleasure. Everything was placed where we had requested without any accidents to persons or valuables. We said our thanks and farewells to this wonderful team and shut the door, exploding with exhausted laughter. Could this really be true, a house of our very own? That night a tired but happy couple climbed the stairs hand in hand.

"Which bedroom shall we use?"

"Let's have a different one every night," I giggled.

Thomas was quick to ask, "Does each room come with a promise?"

"You'll have to wait and see," I replied.

I spent most of my free time wandering around the house, still unable to believe that it was all our own. Every day at work I bored both my kind hearted boss and the customers with news of our house. I was teased and they started to call me Lady Barratt. I felt so shattered with all the excitement and physical exertion of the move. I tried to make light of it, hoping I would soon start to feel like my old self.

Nonetheless, I continued to feel drained of energy. Both Thomas and I were convinced I had been overworking and had been racing about too much but this was not the case. A visit to the doctor confirmed I was pregnant. We were euphoric. I couldn't wait to share our news with my family in my next letter. Mom and Pop

Barratt were overjoyed. Our child would be the first grandchild in both the Brownlow and Barratt families.

I worked in the cafe until Christmas which was almost upon us once again. On my last day I left the cafe laden with baby presents, gifts from my boss and many of the customers. I had to wait for Thomas to come to the cafe on his way home from work, in order to help me carry everything home.

The following Sunday we were invited to the Barratt household to lunch. The house was bursting with the extended family and it was evident that a little scheming was going on. We were both asked to sit down and shut our eyes and keep them shut. Chair legs scraped along the floor, and then we heard some floorboards creaking. The rest of the family obviously found it hard to sit still and keep quiet. Eventually the command to open our eyes was shouted by all and there before us stood the most beautiful, luxurious pram. It was huge. We were bowled over. It was a gift from the family and every single member had contributed. We were both in tears. Why is it that you always cry when you are happy?

Life slowed down a little. I blossomed. Being pregnant suited me. Christmas hurtled towards us at its usual speed. Our forthcoming baby received enough clothes for three babies plus toys by the armful. We would not need to buy a thing, other than a cot. Parcels arrived from England with even more baby clothes. My Mother had made an exquisite shawl and wrapped inside it were petite bags of potpourri made from crushed flower heads from the garden of Willow Cottage. I was determined that our baby would learn to love the countryside as much as I had as a child. When Father read of my pregnancy he wished me well but added that he thought it would have been better, had we waited a little longer. Strange, I thought. Three years wasn't exactly rushing in to it. It was an odd remark to make but I thought he must have had his reasons.

23rd March 1921 arrived and with it Thomas Charles Barratt. He was a beautiful baby. To me, he resembled the Barratts and Thomas was so proud of this and the fact that our wonderful child was perfect in every way.

Life became hectic both day and night. The needs of a baby are paramount and take precedence over everything. Our lives were taken over by this little being who had cast a spell and bewitched us. When he slept I gazed at him in wonder. I became a very protective mother and all I wanted to do was to envelope him in a mantle of love.

Our lives were full, though some news from home was concerning. Mother was far from well. Each letter Father sent to me made reference to medicine that she was taking or the fact that the doctor had changed the prescription. When news such as this reached me I became anxious of the distance between us. It was too formidable to think about.

Thomas Junior, or Tommy, as we now called him, was such a joy. I longed to take him to England and introduce him to the family. I had been coping well with my homesickness but as soon as I became aware of problems my thoughts went to Willow Cottage and my family in Kent.

Thomas loved his new job and was obviously excellent at it as he seemed to be continually promoted from one level to the next. He was clearly well thought of, doing his best for his employers whilst at the same time looking out for his family. His salary steadily rose in line with his promotion, allowing us to pay off our mortgage at a faster rate.

I loved looking after my son but I did miss work and meeting so many people with interesting tales to tell. In truth, I was lonely for adult company. I took the baby for long walks, sometimes to my mother-in-law. She was always so kind to me and I found her very approachable. I think that she must have had a private word with Thomas as one day, out of the blue; he suggested that I had a domestic helper who could also be my companion. It was very thoughtful of him but I felt there was no need and said it would be better if that money went into the Fare Box instead. I think my suggestion made Thomas more aware of my longing for England and my family. It had exposed the feelings that I had tried so hard to suppress. His arms came quickly around me and embracing me he said, "You can go home for a holiday as soon as baby is a little older. He is so tiny for such an arduous journey."

I was delighted and it gave me something to look forward to. The following year was marked off in stages with baby setting the pace. First it was the taking of solids, next sitting up, cutting his first tooth, coming out of nappies; all the normal developments in a baby's life. We seemed to be always clapping him for some achievement or other. On my walks I now spoke to various other pram pushing mothers and that made a big difference to my days. Little Tommy was approaching his second birthday and I intended to plan a party.

I wanted Tommy's birthday to be special and I saw it as an excuse to invite all the Barratt clan plus a few of the pram pushing mothers who had become my friends. I decorated the sitting room with balloons and streamers. As well as all the usual fare I made my first birthday cake using my mother's recipe. I was so proud of my achievements. After everyone had had their fill, we sang Happy Birthday as Tommy attempted to blow out his two candles and then it was time to open presents. Shrieks rang out with every parcel opened. Finally, a beautifully wrapped box was given to Tommy by his Daddy with the instructions that Mummy should help to open it. We tore the paper off together in haste and everybody applauded although they hadn't any idea as to why. It contained a small toy liner plus a note saying, '*You can now book your ticket home.*'

My heart took such a pounding. It was beating so fast. I would never forget this moment, on this special day, for the rest of my life. Thomas hadn't given a hint to anybody of his intentions. The day ended as it had begun with lots of laughter. On giving Thomas his usual goodbye kiss the next morning I hugged him saying, "Thank you darling, thank you, thank you."

Housework was forgotten and Thomas Junior was dressed in record time. I had decided to go to the shipping office right away. I was walking on air. I searched for and found my passport and stowed it away securely in my handbag. Suddenly the reality of what I was about to do brought me to an abrupt halt. I told myself to calm down, sit quietly and think it all through. What would be the best season to travel to England, remembering how cold it can be at sea? I thought I should wait to talk it through with Thomas who I knew would be impressed with my considerations.

I could hardly wait for my husband to return home from work as so many ideas were racing through my head. I had had a wonderful brainwave which wouldn't have come to mind had I followed my first impulse and dashed to the shipping office. Why couldn't we all go to England for Christmas? It is the best time of the year for families. For some reason, I expected opposition from Thomas but it wasn't so. He was all for the idea, as long as, it was all right with his employers and fitted in with his work schedule.

The company was very accommodating and would agree to the vacation, as long as Thomas realised that he would also have to use the following year's leave. We had both forgotten how long the return sea journey would take. I was in seventh heaven and was as excited about this trip home as I had been about our wedding.

Tickets were duly bought for the last week in November and we had one whole month in England to look forward to. Thomas readily accepted that he was using two years leave and was pleased for me. I planned the clothes the three of us were going to take. It wasn't an arduous task and I worked with a happy heart. My next job was to ask Mom and Pop Barratt if they could help us out by watching over the house whilst we were away. How the months dragged from March to November. All I could think of was the voyage home.

I imagined conversations we would have with family and friends. I collected photographs of Thomas Junior at every stage of his development from birth, pictures of the house and some of Thomas's family. I was so proud of our achievements. I didn't feel it was showing off. I had had to put up with so many people saying that it had been wrong to marry and move to another country.

In checking my list of things to do I thought it sensible to get some anti-seasickness pills from the surgery. Our doctor was a lovely man and I had great confidence in him. After examining me and asking me to provide a urine sample, Dr McBride said, "I'd prefer not to prescribe these pills for you Mrs Barratt, as I think you could be pregnant."

I was stunned. Both of us had wanted another baby but certainly not at this stage. I was in such a state that I went directly to Thomas's office for the first time. He, like me, couldn't believe it. I later received a letter from the surgery confirming the pregnancy test was positive. A sorrier household would have been hard to find as neither of us wanted this baby. The trip would have to be cancelled as I couldn’t risk getting violent seasickness in my condition. It was a tremendous disappointment to me.

We gradually picked ourselves up and got on with our lives as best as we could. Christmas came but my pregnancy with all its repercussions marred what should have been a happy event. Everything was an effort but I tried to put on a brave face for my son's sake.

We had so many surplus baby clothes from Tommy that there wasn’t a need to purchase anything, other than a second cot. I felt so guilty about our reaction to this little one inside me. I used to stroke my swollen belly and say sorry, in the hope that he or she could hear me. When my pregnancy started to show we told Tommy that he would be having a little brother or sister. Naturally, at two and a half it seemed a wonderful prospect to him. His delight was a ray of sunshine through the clouds.

Seven

13th June 1924 saw the arrival of our second son. All my fears about how I could love my baby faded the moment I gazed upon his innocent face. Roger Farleigh Barratt had made his entrance into the world. Thomas and I chose the name Roger because we liked it and I chose Farleigh because I thought it would always remind my son of his family roots in Kent. Both Thomas and Tommy adored him instantly and wanted to hold and smother him with kisses.

We were such a happy household. For the first few days of his life Roger Farleigh had visitors galore. Mom and Pop Barratt and the rest of the clan arrived with parcels, even though we had said that we didn't want or need anything. Gifts also arrived from Thomas's colleagues. This little one was so different from his brother. He was quiet and only made little noises when crying. My biggest concern was his disinterest in feeding. I shared my concern with the midwife who advised me to speak to our doctor about it.

A couple of weeks later Thomas arrived home, a little earlier than usual. He looked ashen and stressed. My immediate thought was that he had lost his job. He sat me down, took both of my hands and said, "Esther, you have to be very brave. Today I had a request to attend the surgery and Dr McBride confirmed that Roger Farleigh is deaf and mute."

I wasn't prepared for such abysmal news. I went into instant denial, shouting, screaming and crying. It took a long time for Thomas to calm me down. Even then irrational thoughts entered my head. I wondered if I was being punished for initially not wanting my baby. Apparently, both the doctor and nurse knew shortly after he was born but they had decided to keep it from us until I had recovered from the delivery.

We watched the baby intently to observe his reactions. Both Thomas and I kept testing him and we imagined that we saw him jump when we made a loud noise. Neither of us wanted to accept that the diagnosis was correct. Hospital appointments were made and kept and so began our endless search to find out if anything could be done for him. Little by little we had to agree with the experts' diagnosis. An added anxiety was the suggestion that he could also have slight brain damage. Nothing could console us; we cried, talked and cried again.

An expert in the care of deaf children came to talk to us. She was very understanding and explained that it wasn't the end of the world and that many deaf children went on to achieve marvellous things. She told us that we would be taught ASL (American Sign Language) and would learn to sign alongside Roger Farleigh. Should we find it was all too much for us to cope with, Roger Farleigh could go into a home. That was never a consideration. After she left we sat down and talked of our fears for the future. By the side of us was this beautiful baby, so defenceless, looking up at his Mummy and Daddy. From that special moment we moved forward, treating him, as much as possible, like any other child.

We quickly came to the conclusion that little Tommy had to be told that his baby brother couldn't hear him. We waited until the following weekend when we knew we would all be at home together, enabling us to support Tommy and each other.

"Tommy, your new baby brother is not like other babies. He cannot hear us speaking to him or any other sounds we make. He is deaf, which means we have to make sure he can always see us when we touch or cuddle him. We will all learn to make pictures in the air with our hands so he can understand us."

Tommy listened, asked lots of questions then finally said, "I'm his big brother," before cuddling Roger Farleigh.

Having a deaf child was very demanding. I learned something new every day. Thomas tried to relieve the pressure and took me out for a meal occasionally when Mom and Pop could care for the boys. It took time but our household eventually returned to, as near to normal, as was possible.

Due to our improved finances Thomas decided it was the right time to buy a car. I was amazed as we didn't know anyone amongst our family or friends who owned one. Thomas spent weeks visiting garages and studying brochures. He eventually decided upon a black Model T as they were made by the Ford Motor Company at the works in both Walkerville and Toronto. Assembly line production had reduced the manufacturing costs which made the car more affordable to many more Canadians, including us. Thomas thought it a wise buy at $395.

In the years that followed, most of our friends and family purchased cars. It was decades later that I was to discover, that Henry Ford had confessed in his autobiography that he had told his management team that customers could have their cars painted in any colour they wished, providing it was black. It was nothing to do with Thomas's measured choice or being fashionable. I realised that Thomas had purchased a car because he appreciated that a lot of our time would be spent going back and forth to hospitals and clinics. The car proved to be a wonderful asset. I loved our "Tin Lizzie" as she was affectionately known.

A routine of taking Tommy to school was established and the constant medical appointments for Roger Farleigh were organised around it. I had no help whatsoever running the house. My life was very hectic and a price was paid. My weight plummeted. My clothes no longer concealed the fact that I could see my bones sticking out. In the end I collapsed and was taken to hospital with nervous exhaustion. During my short stay the doctors advised me that I should return when it was convenient, to have my tonsils out. Apparently, the poison from infected tonsils affects your immune system.

Once I had regained some strength, I took heed of the doctor's advice and scheduled my tonsillectomy. This was the one and only time that Thomas wrote to my mother letting her know of my plight. I don't know why he did this, as there was nothing she could do to help. My parents were already stressed by Roger Farleigh's condition and Mother's own health was deteriorating. It was all too much.

Being a mother was my first consideration and I wanted to leave the hospital as quickly as possible to care for my children. I was grateful and relieved when I was finally discharged. Gradually, over the coming year I managed to gain a little weight.

Roger Farleigh steadily accepted his routine. He knew what to do instinctively when he wanted a drink or his nappy changed. Somehow it worked, enabling us to communicate with each other. Everybody who made contact with him was captivated by his wonderful smile and his beautiful big blue eyes.

Thomas's job was very demanding and his hours increased. We were pleased with his advancement but it proved costly in terms of family time. I needed his support now more than ever. Roger Farleigh was walking and needed constant supervision. Little Tommy was virtually always second in line for attention. Having a handicapped brother wasn't easy. It gave me such a guilty conscience that I wasn't being fair to him.

Mom Barratt came often. It helped me when she took the little one for a few hours, as it gave me time to catch up with the housework. There were also times when I needed to visit Tommy's infant school. On one visit the headmistress talked to me about Tommy's behaviour in the classroom. His class teacher had reported that he was constantly demanding attention. The headmistress went on to say that this behaviour was unacceptable. She knew Tommy's brother was deaf but he still had to conform in the classroom like everybody else. She suggested that he needed more attention at home. I listened to her advice and later that evening shared it with Thomas. We decided that we had to do something promptly before things got out of hand. We agreed we would spend more time with him. Bedtime stories were restored and he was given many more cuddles too. We realised that both of us had put the needs of our youngest son before everything else. We were grateful to the school for making us aware of Tommy's plight.

Christmas was approaching again. I seemed to mark my life's progress by this particular time of year. Maybe it was because I had arrived in Canada just before December, when preparations were being made by people I didn't know at the time. My feelings towards this time of year had to change. I had two little sons who would love to see a decorated tree and Christmas lights. I had to start to make this time of year special for the three men in my life.

It seemed strange that Thomas no longer mentioned the possibility of a trip to England, even though Roger Farleigh was growing fast. Strange to say, I really wasn't bothered as my boys were more important to me than anything else.

At the end of January 1928 I received news that my mother had passed away. I was completely devastated. I knew she had been unwell but had not appreciated how serious it was. She had caught a chest infection which turned into pneumonia. No one knew how to console me. Guilt filled my heart and I was full of regret that we had cancelled our trip home. Father's letter assured me that she knew we loved her and that it pleased her to know we were happy and managing to cope with our little family. If you lose your mother when she is old it is agonizing but to lose your mother in her late forties is hard to accept and you question why?

Eventually I came to terms with her death and promised myself that I would start writing to my sister Molly, who would be keeping an eye on Father. Molly had recently married her own childhood sweetheart, Jim, and they now lived only a stone's throw from Willow Cottage. There hadn't been a need to write to her before as she had always read the letters I sent to my parents. It was hard to imagine my father living by himself. Their marriage had been one of love and devotion from the beginning to its end. I really thought they would go on forever. Whatever I became was due to their nurturing and loving care. I hoped my sons would be able to say the same about me.

Father's letters continued to arrive regularly relating the news from Willow Cottage. He often enclosed little brown envelopes containing seeds. Each little packet from home held part of my previous life and would comfort me when I was feeling down.

Months came and went and with them the changing seasons. Both the boys loved Ontario's winter snow, especially when Thomas taught them snow art. He spent hours showing them how to build igloos. For weeks, a little town of giant snow mushrooms became a permanent feature in our back garden.

Mom and Pop Barratt still supported us, helping out whenever they could. I noticed that their visits were not as frequent as they had been previously. I put it down to the fact that the boys were becoming harder work and increasingly heavy to lift. I know I was permanently tired trying to cater for all their needs. Thomas understood, as he too was depleted with all the hours he worked.

Tommy was now doing well in school. His teacher said he had picked up elementary French quickly. I walked from his classroom so proudly and I thought Father will be amazed when I tell him. The day after I'd seen his teacher, Mom Barratt invited us to tea. It was unusual as we normally went at weekends. I asked Thomas if he could join us after work. As his hours at work varied, he said he wasn't sure he could make it but he said he would do his best.

I collected Tommy after school had finished. I tidied him up as little boys always seem to have shirts buttoned up wrongly, ties askew and laces undone. He was no different from the rest of his classmates. We arrived at Mom and Pop Barratt's house to find the table laden with tempting food, the abundant results of Mom's culinary skills. It didn't take long for us to consume most of it. I was as full as could be. Pop Barratt took the boys into the garden for a kick around and Mom poured me another cup of tea.

"I have something to tell you," she said earnestly.

My heart raced. I knew it was something serious. Was she terminally ill or had my father died? It had to be something big. The colour had drained from her face. She had to sit down with my help.

"I don't know how to start," she finally uttered. "I am so sorry."

I could hear my own muffled voice, sounding alarmed.

"What is it? What is it? You can tell me anything."

There was a long pause.

"Thomas is having an affair."

I laughed. I couldn't be hearing right.

"That's ridiculous. It's not possible. He wouldn't dream of it. In any case, he wouldn't have the time he is always working."

She shook her head and I knew then that he wasn't always working. I was in a state of shock. I didn't cry out or scream. Every part of me seemed to have shut down. It was unreal. I could hear the faint sound of Tommy's laughter drifting in from the garden with his little brother's mewing merging with it. They were enjoying Granddad's antics and attention. This couldn't be true. Surely, in a minute I would wake up from this dreadful dream.

"That's not all of it," a remote voice was saying. "The woman is pregnant."

I passed out. I don't remember hitting the floor. I really didn't want to regain consciousness and acknowledge this horror.

Mom Barratt had heard this dreadful news from a friend of hers who thought she already knew about the affair. Thomas was summoned to his parents' house and confronted with these allegations. He admitted it was all true. He was instructed to confess everything to me immediately, and if he didn't, they would tell me themselves. That had been weeks ago but he had lacked the courage and moral fibre to do it, hence the urgent invitation to tea. My poor in-laws were distraught.

Even in my traumatized condition I felt for them. They had only shown love and support to us over the years. Little wonder that Thomas didn't join us for tea. He knew his parents wouldn't wait any longer to tell me of his affair.

My in-laws were so concerned about me and didn't want me to leave but all I wanted to do was to get home. I was in a trance like state as I dressed my little sons. I am sure they sensed something had happened. Silence descended on all three of us as we walked back to the house.

As soon as I opened the front door, I rushed to bath the boys. I read my usual story miming and signing at the same time for Roger Farleigh, kissed them goodnight, adding my usual 'sleep tight,' as I pulled the door to.

I felt nauseous and faint at the thought of what was facing me. I descended the stairs with dread. Hours passed and there was still no sign of Thomas. I looked out of the window countless times. Even the house felt as though it was weighed down with anguish. It was almost midnight when the sound of a key in the lock told me he was home. My instant thought was, I bet he is dreading this. Such a stupid thought for someone with a broken heart who felt her life had ended.

A pathetic man stood in front of me.

"I'm sorry. I don't know what to say."

"Why, why, why?" I screamed, each 'why' louder than the last.

"I don't know."

I was in such a state of turmoil that I went into the kitchen where I automatically made a pot of tea. When I returned, revelations spilled from Thomas's lips. I think he was relieved that he had been found out. Next came the excuses. The affair had started some years ago. He said he felt pushed out by the needs of Roger Farleigh. It was so pathetic. There had been no overtime. The excuses had just allowed him time to be with his mistress. The car hadn't been for us, it had been bought to enable them to get out of town to carry on with their illicit relationship.

It had already started whilst I was in hospital. I wondered how he had managed, as he was supposed to have been looking after the children. He said he had taken them with him and he had relied on Tommy being too young to tell his Mummy or grandparents. It seemed to me that he was unburdening his soul to crucify me. How could he have told me over and over that he loved me, when he had been making love to his mistress? It was all far worse than I could have imagined. Evidently the mistress was his secretary. I recalled him telling me that she was a wonderful person and that she was very efficient. My thoughts were going round and round in circles trying to come to terms with it all. I didn't know what to do. I told him he could stay the night but that I wanted him out for good first thing in the morning and that he had to take all his clothes with him. After telling him this he decided to change his tactics revealing his real worries, which weren't to do with me or the boys.

"I don’t want my employers to find out and would you please plead with my parents to keep it all confidential."

He said he was regretful and didn’t want to leave us. He told me he would end the affair. Thomas showed no apparent concern for his unborn baby, or how his mistress would feel if he abandoned her. My last words of that evening were an outpouring of grief.

"Thomas I forgave you when I discovered you had lied about your age - fourteen years older than me not the seven you claimed. It was hard to accept that you had lied to me even before our marriage, your lie is even on our marriage certificate, but I forgave you. Now more lies and a mistress to boot. How could you do this to me? You didn't even give one thought for what this would do to the children. I cannot forgive and forget this time.

You will sell the house, pay off the mortgage then give me every surplus dollar. It will be needed by your sons when I take them with me to England. I will seek advice immediately from our lawyer about custody of the children and I will never divorce you."

Every day I awoke with the heaviest of hearts and couldn’t see any way forward. I just wished I could run away. During this period the boys were traumatised. They missed their daddy not living at home. Mummy had changed too and was not her usual happy self. I will never know what went on in their little heads, especially Tommy's. Everything was different now. Our friends avoided me; some already knew of the affair whilst others were shocked. In some cases, I was made to feel like the guilty party and I didn't know how to respond.

From the first appointment with the lawyer everything seemed to be stacked against me. Thomas had already instructed him as complainant, which meant instructing a new lawyer to act on my behalf. However, some luck was with me. I was told of a new advocate who had recently arrived from England. I was relieved when he accepted me as his client. His knowledge of immigration law was to help me in the future with custody of the boys.

The allegations that Thomas’s lawyer produced were

unbelievable. They implied I wasn't a good mother. Fees on both sides were mounting up. Thomas was so sure he would win the custody of his sons for two reasons. Firstly, they were Canadians by birthright; secondly, I was a war bride and only Canadian by marriage. He also felt that somehow he was protected because he worked for a government department. It took over a year before the case reached a conclusion but justice prevailed. I won full custody of the boys allowing me to take them out of Canada to England whenever I wished. My only regret was leaving my in-laws. However, they understood completely, as they had given me such support during my legal skirmishes with the Canadian Authorities.

The house sale proved to be another uphill battle. Thomas kept refusing any offers made on the house in order to delay me leaving the country. Once more my lovely in-laws stood firmly behind me. Thomas had borrowed money from them to help him when he was at Victoria College, with the promise that he would pay them back when he could. His parents called in the loan, thus forcing the house sale. Thomas had no choice but to accept this. Mom and Pop Barratt were angels and had done their level best to make amends for their son's devastating behaviour.

Packing was a nightmare. I needed to take most of my home with me as I knew that money would be scarce. Fears about how this would affect Roger Farleigh were uppermost in my mind. I would have to work to support my family. Perhaps my father and sister would be able to help with the children? Molly was already researching schools for the deaf in the Kent area. I needed to find one with a suitable day nursery.

The idea of sending him away from home to board was abhorrent to me. He had already been uprooted from his father and soon he would be leaving his grandparents behind. Thomas had torn our family apart, breaking my heart and spirit in the process. Both my children needed me and some stability in their lives.

Shippers delivered and packed the crates, housing our precious belongings. Both the boys were agitated to see their bicycles and special toys disappearing into boxes. I thought this was the worst time of my life. Every person who witnessed these events said, "Aren't you wonderful and so calm." They didn't see that it was all a facade, inside I was a screaming and gibbering wreck.

My last night in Canada I laid awake feeling I had reached rock bottom but I told myself to hold on and have faith, as nothing could ever be as bad as this again. Now was the time to start anew and face the future ahead. Many offers had come from both family and friends to spend our last night with them, but I declined them all. I thought it would be too traumatic for all three of us and I wanted the boys to be in their familiar beds to reassure them all was well. A story book was their usual end to the day and our last night proved no different. I tried my best to keep them comforted.

At breakfast we were all silent and all three of us were without appetite. A knock came on the door. It was the driver. He was so helpful and sympathetic. He seemed to realise that this was an emotional time for us.

"Have you got the passports, immigration papers and the custodial permits? What about food for the journey and milk for the children?"

His very kindness was almost my undoing as I struggled to keep my composure. We picked up the bags, closed the door and he pushed the keys through the letterbox. We drove away. I didn't even look back. I felt nothing. How could a home that had once been so full of laughter and joy turn into a house full of lies and deceit?

No sooner had I settled the boys into their seats than we arrived at the railway station. The driver escorted us to our carriage which I had booked previously. He made it all so much easier for me by putting the cases up on the high luggage racks and helping the boys to remove their heavy outer clothing. In short, everything a father would do. I shook his hand in farewell, thanked him and asked at the same time how he knew that we needed support? He explained that it was he who had put the note through the door, two days ago, advising me that a car would be collecting us and taking us to the railway station for the start of our journey. I had wrongly thought that it was a gesture from Thomas. It proved to be from my old boss at the cafe, his parting gift to us. What a good friend my former boss turned out to be. His compassion and understanding overwhelmed me.

Both boys enjoyed being on the train. It was all new to

them, their first railway journey. The noise and vibration of the wheels on the track and the occasional whistle made them shriek with laughter. Trains passing in the opposite direction made them almost hysterical. They were entertainment for the other passengers, making the long journey pass more pleasurably. My fears surfaced every moment that I was free from other depressing thoughts. Seeing other passengers put on their coats and remove their cases from the luggage racks told me we were nearing Montreal, our final destination. A fellow traveller helped me with the boys' coats and two men assisted me by lifting the cases down from the rack above. I was grateful for their kindness.

I hailed a porter as soon as I alighted from the train. From that moment on he took care of everything movable, other than the boys. Tommy was acting so grown up that it allowed me to keep an eagle eye on Roger Farleigh. The transfer from the train to the boat was remarkably smooth. I was so relieved. It proved to be an effortless operation, thanks to the steward who took over from the porter. I gave them both a large tip, as they had taken so much stress from me.

When I boarded the ship I had a pleasant surprise. The shipping agents had given me a four berth cabin in third class which meant we had more room. I started to unpack whilst we were still in dock. I felt a little happier as the boys were excited by all the new experiences. We hadn't been in our cabin long when a steward knocked on the door offering to help. This made me feel a bit better knowing I had some support, if only for a short while.

Two hours later, I took both boys up on deck to watch the S.S. Montclare leave the quay. The children thought the boat was colossal but in reality she was only 170m in length. The Montclare's twin funnels with belching grey steam looked very similar to Tommy's toy liner which he was clutching tightly in his hand. The ship had always been one of his favourite toys because it came with a promise from his father of a voyage to England. Tommy's birthday had been one the happiest days of my life but now I felt the finality of our abandonment by Thomas. Tears coursed down my cheeks at this bitter sweet moment.

We found a spot on deck by one of the life boat stations. Lots of people were waving farewell and some were crying at the thought of leaving their loved ones. The next quay we would see would be Southampton. It wasn't too long before I began to feel light headed and nauseous with seasickness. I couldn't believe it as we had hardly moved. I came to the conclusion that it was the sound and throb of the turbines rather than the sea itself which had triggered me off.

There was much for the boys to explore on board the ship. It was very different from my first journey. We dined at our reserved table which was allocated to us for the entire voyage. Once I had got my sea legs I was able to relax a little. I was temporarily freed from my worries for a while, which meant I could watch over the boys and entertain them. Roger Farleigh needed my vigilance constantly. Other little children on board didn't understand, initially, that he couldn't hear them. Roger Farleigh would run up to them and tug at their clothes to make them look at his face; they would then call out to their mothers for help. It only took a couple of days for the word to spread to the other passengers on our deck that he was deaf. From then on it was never a problem. In fact, he became spoilt by other little children trying to baby him, which he loved.Crew members would ask my permission to hoist him aloft on to their shoulders and would walk around the decks with little Tommy following in their footsteps.

At night I didn't leave the cabin. Both the boys slept well. I found this time peaceful and invaluable as it was my thinking time. One night I started to make plans for our future but I realised it was impossible. Everything depended on Roger Farleigh's school. Tommy could go to a school anywhere but schools for the deaf were few and far between.

However hard I tried, my thoughts meandered back to the past. I kept recalling conversations I had had with Thomas. Why hadn't I guessed about the affair? I had had so many clues. I had praised Thomas for his choice of birthday presents and surprises on anniversaries. Everything was always beautifully wrapped with matching ribbons. It's the thing you do when the recipient is special to you. It now hurt me to realise that Thomas's mistress had probably not only chosen the presents but had wrapped them too. I felt that the pain and humiliation of this betrayal would never leave me.

I started reading again to take my mind off things I would prefer to forget. It really helped me and I found solace in a couple of autobiographies of famous people who had achieved wonderful things in their lives.

The next morning I was surprised by a request from the captain to take tea with him. I was very apprehensive because I couldn't work out why I had been invited. Perhaps there was a problem? I couldn’t recall having done anything that would concern a ship’s captain. We arrived at the appointed time. The captain requested a tray of tea and cakes plus glasses of milk for the boys. He asked if I was satisfied with our cabin and wanted to know if the stewards were looking after our needs. He waited until I got up to go before he handed me a large envelope.

"This was left for you at the shipping agents and I was requested to hand it to you when we were at sea."

I thought it might be more documents full of legal jargon from Thomas’s lawyer. I couldn't think of another explanation. I was intrigued as it was such a thick brown envelope. I finally opened it when we returned to the privacy of our cabin. I was astonished to find it was full of money. I gasped aloud when I saw the amount.

It was from Mom and Pop Barratt. An accompanying letter was enclosed with the money. They explained that Thomas had cleared his loan and he had repaid his debt to them in full. They didn’t want the money but realised it would go a long way towards helping me get back on my feet. I stood quietly holding their letter, tears streaming from my eyes. They knew that I wouldn't have accepted the money in Canada. It was a sizeable amount, certainly enough to see us through the first difficult months. I was so thankful for the love they had shown me from the first moment I had met them.

I continued to remain in the cabin at night whilst the boys slept. I liked resting in my bunk in the dark. One night I came to the conclusion that it was time for me to try and put things behind me. My brain seemed to respond by letting go all my negative thoughts and sleep came easily to me that night.

I awoke to Tommy's cries of, "Mummy wake up," whilst Roger Farleigh pulled at my nightgown, which was his way of saying the same thing. I felt refreshed after my good night's sleep. I hugged both the boys and pulled them into my bunk for cuddles. The world looked inviting again. That morning as I dressed I felt as if a weight had been lifted from my shoulders and I was in good spirits. The boys laughed at me. I had deliberately put my clothing on back to front with my left shoe on the right foot. It was a long time since I had played the fool with the children and I felt this was a positive sign of my progress.

Tommy asked me, "Mummy why do you call me Tommy? You call Roger Farleigh two names."

I was surprised that he was obviously not happy about it.

"My name is Thomas Charles"

"Well, we have two Thomases in our family and we thought that Tommy sounded nice and we would know which one to call when we needed you. If you want to change it, you can. That's not a problem."

"I like Tommy, Mummy."

"In that case we will keep to that and call your brother Roger."

I had learned a lesson. Never make assumptions about children's likes and dislikes or their sense of fairness. A happy trio went in to breakfast, Mummy, Tommy and Roger.

I was always amazed at the workings of the human psyche and intrigued by the way people dealt with the situation life presents to them, such as moments of despair, financial pressure, the loss of loved ones and so on. These pressures often appear unsolvable and take their toll on us all. During the past year, I had had my fair share of trauma and I was nearly at breaking point but somehow on the voyage home, my little boys showed me there was a way forward; they were my future. Any other concerns not related to the boys and me were of no consequence. I came to realise that together we would be able to face whatever lay ahead.

Each day brought some form of excitement or new experience that we all enjoyed and we noticed it was getting warmer. Our arrival was scheduled for the fourteenth of June and the Montclare was keeping good time.

It was interesting to observe how the other passengers had changed too. They had also become relaxed and enquired of each other, 'Where have you come from? or Where are you going?'

I told the boys that when we docked at Southampton they would have to watch out for Auntie Molly, Uncle Jim, her husband, and their two children. I knew Father wouldn't be able to undertake the journey because Molly had already prepared me. She had told me that he had become very frail since Mother had died.

During the last twenty four hours of the journey I tried to be a calm mother but I found it very difficult because my thoughts kept racing ahead. I was already in Willow Cottage unpacking our trunks. The last day on board was really hectic but packing was pleasurable, unlike before. Our heavy Canadian padded coats were packed away and we hung up our lighter ones in readiness for our arrival and the English summer. Whilst I worked out how to get everything back in the trunks, the boys were really animated, jumping up and down all over the cabin. Roger didn't need to speak his facial expressions said it all. Tommy was so excited that I had to change his pants.

Breakfast was a hurried affair, not only for us, but for others too. Most passengers wanted a position close to the rails in order to spot their relatives on the quay. We thought that by hurrying breakfast we would get the best positions. I did miss having a husband with me. Often it was for the minor routines of the day like the boys having to accompany me on my visits to the deck lavatory but now I missed him for his company, and to share my exhilaration.

Clutching both boys tightly by the hands we managed to squeeze our way through the crowds and we found a rail position in the middle of the deck. Familiar sounds filled the air. Cranes, creaking crates banging as they were swung high into the air before being dumped onto the quayside for the awaiting stevedores. It was a different feeling of excitement to that which I had felt when I arrived in Canada. Now I had no fear of the unknown. I glanced up to the upper deck where the Captain was stationed. He looked particularly impressive in his uniform and stood in a fixed position, surveying all that was going on around him. We were so far below him that he appeared extraordinarily small, making him bear a resemblance to one of Tommy's toy model figures. There were so many people lining the quay awaiting their families. I doubted we would spot ours. Molly had made the suggestion that we should stand as close as possible to one of the gangplanks when we disembarked and to stay there until they found us. I wasn't so sure that this was a good idea but all my worries dissolved when I spotted Molly and Jim with their two children, Jimmy and Clare. The commotion around us was deafening. We shrieked at each other without understanding a word. My heart was beating rapidly. We were home on schedule, 14th June 1929.

We gathered speed running down the gang plank towards Molly. I am sure that the boys' little feet left the ground. We hugged, cried and uttered words I cannot recall and then descended into complete silence. The nine years or so, during which time we hadn't seen each other, vanished into thin air. Both boys clutched each other and their faces betrayed their unhappiness. I'm sure my constantly changing emotions had affected them. I dropped to the ground and hugged them and tried to assure them that all was well. I then tried to cheer them up by telling them that they now had cousins to play with but for the first time in their short lives I was unable to console them.

We made the journey to Kent with them still subdued and very distressed. Jimmy and Clare were overwhelmed too.

Eight

Willow Cottage was as I remembered. Both the boys had slipped into sleep amidst the tears and Jim had carried them upstairs to their bedroom, laying them fully clothed on their beds. I took a closer look at Father. He had become so fragile. Clearly, my mother's death had dented his wonderful spirit. I looked around the cottage and all the things that I was so familiar with such as Mother's Welsh dresser and even the shabby sofa, appeared smaller than I remembered. In Canada everything was so much larger or appeared so.

I took the opportunity to wander outside to enjoy the garden. Much had changed. It had become a little overgrown. Bind weed had reared its ugly head and was entwined around fruit bushes as well as pushing its way through the paths. It was doing its best to gain control of the honey suckle which clambered through the apple tree. Gardens are such a haven but if you neglect them they are also unforgiving. I sat on the old wooden bench at the end of the path. Its familiar smooth, worn surface was comforting. I sobbed and sobbed. I felt I had emigrated in reverse. I suddenly missed Thomas's love and strength. I was also very scared about the future.

Father's voice filtered through my howls of pain. "Girlie, girlie, let it all come out. You need this time for yourself."

I cried uncontrollably for what seemed like a very long time. With Father's arms still around me we returned along the old cobbled path. Sleep and my own childhood bed awaited me. I knew I would be ready for tomorrow.

Next morning we all looked so much better. Tommy and Roger were all smiles as they ran out to explore the garden and Father didn't look quite so frail. I decided to use my first day at home to take stock and think about our immediate future. Father had invited us to stay at Willow Cottage until I was able to sort out schools for both boys.

It was imperative for me to find a job to support us. Thomas had been ordered by the court to give us a part of his income to ensure that we would be able to survive. I had already decided to leave it in the bank in Canada. It would enable the boys to see their father when they were a little older or I could use it if we became destitute. I spent the day unpacking. All the clothes smelled slightly damp. Socks had little holes in them and buttons were missing from shirts. Mending them was therapeutic for me. It was the start of me putting my house in order.

I awoke the next morning with a sense of needing to achieve something. All three of our faces looked more relaxed as we ate our porridge and it raised my spirits and gave me hope. Molly had volunteered to take care of the boys and entertain them for the day. It would be a good way for them all to get to know each other. Signing was totally bewildering to her so Tommy helped her communicate with Roger. Although the boys hadn't met their aunt before they instinctively trusted her.

I entered the bathroom knowing I needed to look at my best before looking for work. The past year or so had been horrendous and had taken its toll. My self esteem was at its lowest. I was forever thinking, what had I done wrong? Now was the time to say to myself in one word - nothing. You are a good woman, intelligent and attractive; now get on with your life.

I left the house with a sense of purpose, a straight back and my head held high. I was wearing a smart suit and my shoes were gleaming. Father's comment of, "You look wonderful," also helped me on my way.

As I walked down the road it dawned on me that until I had information about a special school for Roger any search for a job would be futile. I had always had a tendency to rush in to things and I would need to bear that in mind in the future. The District Education Committee had to be my first port of call. Molly had found out that they would certainly be able to point me in the right direction.

I was fortunate to see a member of staff who kindly arranged for me to be seen immediately. I felt this had to be a good sign. People in the office were very helpful and promised to do all that they could to help me.

The following week I was interviewed regarding Roger's special needs. The first proposition from the education authority was to ask if I would consider residential provision for Roger. My immediate answer was a definite no. In any case, my decision could only be made after a full assessment had been carried out by the medical team.

I used my walk home to mull things over. I realised then what a miracle it was that Mom and Pop Barratt had given us that extra money. We would be able to survive for a few months or so. My head was still reeling from all the in depth questions I had been asked at the interview. Everything I said had been noted and written down. When I returned home to Willow Cottage I told Father that no decisions could be made until Roger had had a medical examination.

Each day after taking Tommy to school I pottered in the garden with little Roger beside me. I was also able to assist Molly by keeping Willow Cottage in order, giving her time for her own family. Roger relished waiting with me outside Tommy's school when we collected him at home time. I noticed that he loved the attention of the little children who ran up to him in the playground and he would smile at the teachers who always waved to him.

We anxiously awaited a letter from the Education Department about Roger's medical assessment. We received one in August informing us that the appointment was for 4th September. I was both fearful and relieved. It felt like a long time to wait so I made a game out of it with Roger crossing off the days on the calendar.

4th September duly arrived. I had been advised that it would be a lengthy examination and to take food and drink sufficient for the day. I was able to stay with Roger for most of the time. He had only been shown kindness by doctors over the four years of his life. He had no fear, which made it so much easier for me. Even when they requested me to leave the room Roger was still smiling. He was so happy to be in their care but for me each minute we were apart felt like hours. At last I was called in to hear the results of their assessment. Roger was still happy, playing with the educational toys that had been given to him. The specialist asked me quietly to take a seat.

"Mrs Barratt, It's not good news I'm afraid. I regret to tell you, your child is not only deaf, he is also mentally retarded."

I heard these words as if from afar. Deep down I already knew. I had kept the knowledge of my child's imperfections locked away in my heart. I remembered only too well the concerns of both the doctor and the midwife at Roger's birth.

I was also informed that Roger would have to attend a residential school as he required the expert care of professionals. Should I disagree I would condemn him to a silent world of isolation and frustration. There could only be one answer for my dearest child. He must have the best possible care. We left the hospital late in the afternoon. Roger was still his cheerful self but I was a heartbroken mother.

On our arrival home Molly was waiting at the door to greet us. She had kindly collected Tommy from school when she picked up Jimmy and Clare. She and the children wanted to stay at the cottage with Tommy and Father until I arrived home with the news. I was shocked to find that both she and Father had already guessed Roger's condition was far more serious than I was letting on. Nothing is as blinkered as a mother's love.

St Mary's residential school found a place for Roger within two months. Most fortunate for us, the school was in Margate and although fifty miles from our home we could visit with not too much trouble. Rules only allowed one visit per week, on a Sunday. I wasn't happy with this but the reason given to me was that the children would become unsettled with more frequent visits. I was eventually to concede that they were right.

Roger settled in relatively quickly and made lots of new friends. When we visited him, it didn't take long for him to get bored with us. He would then focus his attention on his new brothers and sisters. It hurt at first but at the same time lessened the feeling of betrayal that lived within me.

Tommy was progressing and doing well at his new elementary school. He too had had to move on from the devastation of the custody battle and being apart from his father and little brother. He had experienced so much upheaval in his life. He had to endure settling in to a new country, family and school. He had done well to adapt so readily.

With both boys established at their respective schools, I had to rethink my own employment. I would have thought it impossible that Roger would have settled so well into his new home. I tried not to feel guilty that the quality of mine and Tommy's life had greatly improved. We were both sleeping much better and I was able to support my eldest son at school events. His friends were able to come to tea and play. In short a normal life.

Everything began to feel different. Father had become stronger and Molly loved having her sister and family nearby. I was more relaxed. This wasn't because Roger was at residential school but more to do with the passage of time. We were no longer visitors on holiday. Thomas and my love for him was gradually fading into the past.

Weeks went by and the daily business of searching for a job was proving fruitless and very discouraging. I diligently kept trying and in due course out of the numerous applications, three companies replied favourably within the same week. They looked promising and all three companies called me for interviews.

In every case, as soon as I was questioned about my family commitments, the company concerned brought the interview to a swift conclusion. Roger was at boarding school and Tommy had both his auntie and grandfather to care for him, so no problem existed. I didn't ever get a chance to present the facts. I was so dejected and also felt very concerned about my finances which were dwindling at a rapid pace. My last interview also failed and I became frantic and very worried. I could feel panic spreading through my body. I told myself, stop, take a break, find a cafe, sit down and relax with a cup of tea then think about your next move.I knew there was a Lyon's tea shop two streets away and promptly headed in that direction. On entering the cafe a woman smiled at me.

"Why don't you sit here?"

I was about to decline when I looked again at her face and realised that she was an older version of the office junior from my pre-war company. I didn't get to know her well because I had enlisted in the Air Force and left. I did however recall her name was Joyce.

We sat talking and I before I knew it I had spilled out my life story from joining the WRAFs to my present predicament. She held my hand and I could feel her empathy. Tears streamed down my face. It was such a release. I didn't have to pretend to be strong, I could be myself. When I was composed again she asked if I felt better for unburdening myself. I said I felt much better and thanked her. My head had stopped pounding and the shaking had stilled.

Next I was hearing words spill from her lips that I couldn't believe.

"I will offer you a job. We have a vacancy in the office. You're in luck Esther, one of the girls leaves next week. She's getting married and her husband wants her to give up work. By the way, I'm now the office manageress." I started to cry again and this time she joined me but the tears were of joy and sheer disbelief. Not only had I been offered a job but it was with my old company. I wouldn't have to explain about the children or being separated. The 4.40 train from Charing Cross couldn't go fast enough for me. I wanted to get home quickly to share my good news.

Work developed in to a regular pattern. Every week-end was free which enabled me to visit Roger. My office colleagues were a good bunch and at long last I had adult friends again. They would share with me all their news about their families and I was able to pass on so much of it in my letters to Mom and Pop Barratt. My contact with them was important for me and the children. I really loved my in-laws. They would always be in our lives, a constant reminder of our Canadian life and family. The Barratts had supported us without question through good and bad times. Now their love for us extended across the ocean and they still continued to support us financially.

Roger remained happy in his surroundings. It was difficult to believe that this little child was so handi-capped. Tommy grew at such a pace he constantly needed larger clothing as well as new shoes.

My job was going well. I had had several wage increases in a short space of time which made me feel valued and appreciated. Father loved us living with him so there was no added encumbrance of finding other accommodation. His beloved garden was even returning to its former glory. It was no longer an obligation to either of us. We both tackled the outside jobs together. I learned so much from him. Apart from the normal gardening routines of planting, pruning etc. I became an expert at using a saw and creosoting fences.

My colleagues at work included me in many of their social functions. Once, I was asked out by a friend of a friend. I reluctantly agreed and took myself off to Maidstone to seek a selective store to buy a new outfit for the occasion. I browsed through frocks for ages but eventually bought a very smart suit plus the highest of high heeled shoes that I could find. They were the height of fashion at the time. If my memory serves me correctly the department store in the High Street was called Blake and Son.

The special evening arrived and I felt like a young girl going on her first date. I gazed in the mirror after I had dressed and put on my makeup and said out loud, "You look great girl."

I walked carefully down the stairs in my new high heels. Father looked up from his newspaper and complemented me, "You look gorgeous. I wish I was taking you out." I felt good about myself and this coupled with Father's flattering remark made me think it was a good omen for an excellent night ahead.

However, the evening was disastrous. My 'date' was uncomfortable with the fact that I had been married and was now separated with two children. It seemed to terrify him. He couldn’t handle the situation or me. On the one hand he loved the idea of being with an experienced woman, (I think he thought he had got it made) but on the other hand he didn't know where to start. It was embarrassing for both of us. I left as soon as I was able without eating a thing that had been ordered. I had only sipped from the glass of water that was provided on the table. I felt humiliated and degraded. It was obvious I had sent out the wrong signal somehow.

I felt this disaster entitled me to treat myself to a taxi.On the way home I laughed aloud and wondered how much the bill had come to, for nothing in return? It must have taught him a lesson for it had me. Never again, I thought.

After retiring to bed I had the giggles as the feeling of being rejected left me and I thought, 'Well my man, you will never know your loss.' With that in my mind I fell asleep smiling.

Nine

Occasionally one of my friends would visit in the evening and we would play records. Father had bought me a wind up gramophone. He called it that 'confounded contraption.' On one of these evenings I opened the door to my friend, as I thought, but there stood Thomas James Barratt as well.

"Oh my God. What the hell are you doing here?" I was then stunned into complete silence. My mouth became so dry and my heart beat so rapidly it echoed through my head. My friend who had actually rung the bell could see that I was in a predicament and rushed back down the path, calling over her shoulder, "See you in the morning Esther."

This shabby, pallid man didn't even look like the Thomas I had known. It could only have been a couple of minutes but it seemed like an eternity before I asked him again,

"Why are you here?"

All he could say was, "Forgive me. I'm truly sorry.

Can I come in?"

Thoughts rushed through my head - the shock could kill Father and what about Tommy? He was in bed thank goodness. I shut the door on Thomas, telling him to wait until I broke the news to Father, who like me, found it hard to believe. We both realised that we couldn't keep him standing forever on the door step so we invited Thomas in without too much grace. Father stood by my side as protector then calmly walked over to the dresser, poured two small brandies, and gave one to Thomas. As Father wasn't a drinker I knew that he was playing for time and plucking up courage, preparing for whatever was about to come.

It was well over an hour before Thomas was composed enough to speak coherently. Apparently, he had been in England for a week and was sleeping rough after hitchhiking from Southampton. What a deplorable situation to be in after working as a professional and owning his own house. Once Father had seen that Thomas had no intention of harming me or Tommy he retreated upstairs and said, "I am only a call away should you need me."

Thomas's account took all night to tell. After 2 a.m. I got beyond the point of tiredness. Every so often I called a halt to what was being said to make a pot of tea and some toast to sustain us.

Thomas continued, "My mother and father will have nothing to do with me."

This, I already knew. At that stage he didn't realise

that we were in close contact with his parents. Thomas was no different from other men who had cheated on their wives. He said that he was so sorry and he hadn't meant for things to get so out of hand.

"Please find it in your heart to forgive me Esther."

All this pleading was wasted emotion as far as I was concerned. The tears rolling down his cheeks did not distress me, only anger welled up into my heart. How dare he do this? I had moved on and had slowly recovered from unbearable pain, all of which he had caused.

Much more was to follow. His girlfriend had had an abortion blaming her decision on him and the attitude of his family towards her. Her own family had disowned her when they had discovered that Thomas was a married man with two sons, one of whom was handicapped. She and Thomas had parted within six months. I quickly worked out that Thomas must have broken up with his mistress before I had left for England. Why hadn't he told me then? He wouldn't admit to anything and then promptly went on to declare that he couldn’t start any other relationship because of the love he still felt for me. None of the explanations or reasons for his behaviour moved me or disturbed my conscience. At this stage he hadn’t even mentioned our two beloved sons.

After all the hours of talking Father offered Thomas breakfast as it was obvious that he hadn’t eaten properly for some time and was without money. I told him that he would have to go before Tommy got up to get ready for school. Although Tommy was now ten years old I didn't think he would recognise his father in his present state but I didn’t want to take that chance. Father escorted Thomas to the gate and as I watched them walk down the front path, I saw him give some money to Thomas.

As soon as Tommy entered the school playground I rushed to Molly's house to arrange for her to collect him after school. It would give me some much needed time. She too found it all unbelievable and commented, "Things like this only happen to other people or in novels. I can't believe Thomas had the audacity to turn up unannounced after all he's put you through. The impertinence of the man."

I returned home and managed to sleep for a couple of hours but I didn't wake refreshed. My sleep was disturbed by constantly replaying the events of the previous night. What was I supposed to do or say to Thomas on his return? All is forgiven, come home and we will resume life from where we left off? All the love I once felt for him had vanished from me. I didn’t even feel affection. What turmoil he had now placed me in and there wasn’t a straightforward solution. My father, a committed Christian, was dismayed when I said that I had no forgiveness in me for the father of my children.

"Always give someone a little glimmer of hope, even if you can’t forgive them," he urged me.

I couldn’t give Thomas anything. My heart was as cold and heavy as marble.

Thomas looked a little better on his return. Father’s money had paid for bed and breakfast for the week ahead.

He thanked Father and told him that he would repay him when he found work. Hearing that comment caused me immense concern as I wondered what he meant by it? We agreed that he wouldn't return for at least a week to give me time to tell Tommy that his daddy was coming on holiday from Canada to see his two lovely boys.

The week passed quickly and during that time Thomas had posted several notes through the letter box. They all conveyed excuse after excuse and were pleading his cause. None of the letters moved me. In fact it had the opposite affect. How dare he turn our lives upside down again.

Tommy was incredibly excited that his father was coming from Canada especially to see him and his little brother the following weekend. I had that sinking feeling that it was a huge mistake to allow Thomas to see the boys.The designated Sunday arrived for Thomas's visit. I was very edgy, not from the visit per se but from the issues that could develop afterwards. Tommy was over excited. Every few minutes he ran to the window to look out for him. Finally, Thomas walked towards the gate where Tommy was standing, waiting to greet him. Children are so unpredictable. As soon as Tommy saw his father he ran back to me and peered back tentatively at Thomas. We left him to greet his father in his own time. Father joined us for coffee and the tension between us all was palpable. At the end of the morning I served a light lunch. Tommy sat next to his father. After our meal we had to face the visit to Roger. Thomas asked me why I wasn't adding Farleigh to Roger's name anymore. It took a few minutes to explain that Tommy had decided that he would prefer it, if he and his brother were treated the same and called by their first names only.

We finally set off to Margate to see our youngest son. I don't know what Thomas was expecting but after ten minutes I could see he was shaken when Roger did his usual disappearing act. He was our same little cheerful boy but he quickly got bored with us and wanted to go off in search of his friends' company. Thomas obviously appreciated that Roger would have grown but couldn't accept that he had distanced us in favour of his new family. Thomas broke down and was distraught at this new discovery.

I waited until we had left the school before I related the outcome of Roger's medical assessment. I explained to Thomas that for Roger to be happy and well cared for, he would need the constant assistance of professionals. I imagined that Thomas felt guilty and that this weighed heavily upon him, especially when added to all the other emotions that he was experiencing that day. However, these feelings were short lived and he steered the situation around to thinking about what was best for him. Obviously, that would be a return to a reunited family. This was the moment I declared my intentions of never playing the role of happy families with him again.

More news was to ensue when we arrived home and it wasn't what I wanted to hear. It was so outrageous that I was absolutely flabbergasted when Thomas suggested, "I will find a good job here and get a house so that the boys can visit me when they like."

Worse was to come. Thomas announced that his work contract in Canada had been terminated because of his unreasonable behaviour, which meant that his pension rights had gone too. I was also to lose the allowance that the Canadian court had awarded me.

I couldn't wait to see him leave the house. His parting words to me that evening were, "See you next Sunday." I never wanted to see him again. Every word that he had said was like a dagger entering my heart. I had told myself that things couldn't get any worse but they just had. Yet again, Thomas was only considering himself. He wanted a cosy home with a loving wife and two sons who adored him. I just wanted one thing, to get him out of our lives forever.

I had to seek legal advice for a second time. Lawyers were expensive and that concerned me greatly. My sister and her husband came to Willow Cottage one night to join Father and me for supper and a family conference. Both Molly and Jim offered me their life savings and Father wanted to give me the money that he intended to leave me as my legacy. Such loving support for me was overwhelming.

A colleague at work recommended me to a lawyer who specialised in family and marital law. I booked an hour's consultation for the following Friday. I wanted to be armed with advice before the next Sunday visit from Thomas. Had the fee been double, every penny of it would have been well spent. It turned out that all the terms of the custody agreement made in Canada still applied in the English courts. Thomas's present behaviour and lack of employment supported the concerns I had about his visitation rights to the boys. Six months later Thomas was granted visiting rights of once a week providing he was sober and solvent.

Thomas didn't return to Willow Cottage ever again. Father had made it clear to him on his second visit that cups of coffee and meals were not on offer to unwelcome guests. A few weeks passed with Thomas seeing Roger at the same time as Tommy and me. Roger always went off to his friends whilst Tommy stood silently close to my side. One Sunday proved to be Thomas's undoing. He arrived to see the boys in a drunken state. That was the last visit allowed by officialdom.

Letters continued to be posted through our letterbox, usually at night, so that we couldn't challenge Thomas. The notes were always begging for forgiveness with the same excuses repeated time after time. Fortunately, we didn't have the added worry that Tommy would be affected by his father's absence as he thought his daddy had returned to Canada after his holiday. In some ways, it was not surprising to us, that as time went by Tommy mentioned his father less and less.

From time to time various friends spotted Thomas in Maidstone, usually drunk and unkempt. We found it hard to understand that he hadn't returned to Canada. It could have been the lack of money. Conversely, he had worked his passage on his outward journey so why hadn't he done the same in reverse? Naturally, had he presented himself to the shipping agents in his usual drunken condition he would have been rejected. It would have been exactly the same had he applied as a fare paying passenger. Maritime laws were very strict. Thomas needed to sort his life out. Britain was in the midst of the Great Depression and many hard working, law abiding citizens were out of work and struggling to survive.

The Great Slump, as it was also known in the 1930s, was Britain's largest economic depression of the 20th century. Britain's world trade fell by a half and the output of heavy industry by a third. Employment plunged and at its worse in the summer of 1932, 3.5 million people were unemployed and many more were only in part time employment.

Over the course of several years, some members of the family and the odd friend would occasionally come across Thomas who was usually intoxicated and always in a fifthly, uncared for state. What a waste of a life. His thrilling, illicit love affair coupled with the world's failing economy had had disastrous consequences for him.

Ten

It was a misty day in February 1936. It had begun like any other. Father and Tommy were eating their breakfast whilst I grilled my usual piece of toast, eating it as I waited on the two of them. A loud knock came from the front door. It was so loud and insistent that I rushed towards it shouting, "I'm coming."

I opened the door as fast as I could. A sombre looking policeman stood on the threshold and asked if he could come in as he wished to talk to me. I invited him into the sitting room. Nothing prepared me for what he was going to say next. Thomas was dead. He had committed suicide. It was a bolt from the blue and I sank into the nearest chair with sheer disbelief. He had gassed himself and had left a note for Tommy. He hadn't been able to rise above the degradation. My thoughts immediately went to the Barratts. How would I be able to tell his parents? It was as though the constable had read my thoughts.

"The Canadian Embassy has informed his parents. Your sons are named as next of kin."

It was all unreal. My biggest concern was working out how I was going to break the news to Tommy. He was still eating his breakfast, unaware of what was unfolding in the sitting room.

I showed the police constable out of the house then walked straight back into the kitchen to break the news. Fortunately, Tommy was well aware of his father's circumstances and that he had remained in England. It had become necessary to tell him when he started to correspond with his grandparents. Neither Tommy nor I ever felt the need to enlighten them about the downfall of their son. Although Tommy was now fifteen and a young man, his reaction to his father's death astounded me. He told me that it was what he had expected to happen eventually. "I'm not surprised Ma. How long could he have gone on living as he was?"

Roger was obviously totally oblivious of what had happened. His insular world remained the same to him, nothing bad ever intruded. I was allowed an extra visit to see him. I just hugged him tightly and remembered the times long ago when his daddy had loved him.

The police informed me that Thomas had been living in Union Road in Clapham at the time of his death. I had still thought of him as living in Maidstone. We decided on a quiet funeral with just Tommy and me attending. It wasn't to prove as simple as we first thought. I don't think many people realise that there is a protocol that has to be observed when burying people. Any person taking their own life or innocent stillborn babies cannot be buried in consecrated ground.

I was horrified by this discovery. Usually the person committing this act is very desperate or unbalanced, whatever the case, they are sick. I was infuriated with the authorities and the church that had sanctioned these rules. The land that the rules applied to was considered consecrated to God. For me He was the greatest forgiver of all. I mangaged to find a way around this anomaly. I purchased a plot of land in Streatham cemetery and Thomas was interred with the respect due to any human being. In the future I intended to join with others in a campaign for the church hierarchy to rescind this particular piece of legislation.

Tommy's letter from his father requested that he look after me and with it he enclosed a shilling. It saddened me to remember how much we were in love at the beginning. When somebody close to you dies you feel sorrow at their passing and usually relief if they were suffering. A suicide leaves a different sense of loss, perhaps it is guilt that you were unable to help but in my case all I felt was indifference.

Mom and Pop Barratt received the news about the loss of their son much better than I had thought. Their letter said that as there had been no contact with Thomas for such a long time they had already suffered his loss years beforehand. That touched my heart and for the first time I cried for Thomas's death and his wasted life.

I thought that life would resume its familiar pattern but this would prove to be so wrong. I had felt no love for

Thomas for many years and yet something seemed missing from my life after his death. For so long I had had concerns about his way of life. Every day I had thought about him, if only for a moment or two. I had told myself that these thoughts were unnecessary and shouldn't exist and that time would eventually erase him from my memory.

Tommy changed from a carefree boy into a more serious young man. The manner of his father's death had a profound effect on him. The enormity of any person taking their own life was hard for him to understand. He found the letter left to him with the enclosed shilling, a burden to carry. So much so that he sought to find reasons to justify his father's actions. Naturally I was blamed. His accusation was that, had I given Thomas another chance it might have prevented his suicide. The injustice of this weighed me down. Little did he realise that I had already judged myself. Life wasn't fair. I felt so depleted with all the unfair criticism from my son. When would it end for me and what would it take to regain my inner peace? I decided to talk to my father. I waited until Tommy had gone to bed. Panic swept over me, what would I do should Father hold the same opinion as Tommy? I didn't know where to begin.

Father with his usual wisdom started the discussion for me. How well he knew his daughter. He had already seen the different paths that Tommy and I were taking. He knew I had not given Tommy the real reason for leaving Canada and he was aware that Tommy blamed me for his father's suicide. Father told me to be patient and that Tommy would perhaps ask more searching questions when he was mature enough to deal with with the answers. I wept as I listened to his words. He was the keeper of all our secrets, both good and bad. My father continued to support us every day until we began to see more clearly.

Sunday visits to Roger resumed their regular pattern. His sunny nature combined with his innocence was uplifting during these difficult times. On our arrival he would rush to greet us to claim his gifts of comics and sweets. I found it was the bright coloured pictures in the comics that excited him most. Sometimes he would accept a kiss and a cuddle but most times he would push me away. Tommy would stick his hand out to Roger as if to shake hands with him but was never quite able to complete the action before Roger ran away. It was evident to me that Roger had reached his potential. He was now eleven years old but behaved more like a five or six year old. I felt saddened but at the same time I could see and feel that my smiling boy was happy in his own little world.

As we walked home Tommy told me he had been doing a lot of thinking.

"You can add Roger's second name now, if you like. I will call myself Thomas as it sounds more adult."

My first reaction was to accept that Tommy was now fifteen years old and had moved on in his own way. Then after thinking about it for a few minutes I eventually answered him.

"You can call yourself Thomas if you wish but Roger's name is to stay as it is."

I certainly had mixed feelings but it wasn't to do with Tommy reverting to his full name. It was the way he was beginning to assert himself.

It was only a few days later that I received a letter from Thomas's school requesting my presence to discuss his attitude. He had been discourteous to both staff and pupils. Up until this time I had always been proud of his achievements. Starting with his scholarship he had progressed through each year's exams with first class results and was known for his caring attitude. If there were any fights between other boys, Tommy was always the one to placate either side. This request filled me with trepidation.

I was interviewed by the headmaster as well as the form teacher. They were kind and their only concern was to help Tommy through this difficult period. On my arrival home Tommy or Thomas as he now preferred, had nothing to fear resulting from my visit to the school. I had no negative words to relate, only to tell him that his headmaster and teacher were there for him should he need somebody to talk to. However, his behaviour and attitude had to change if he wanted to progress at school.

Neither of the boys was ever told about their father's affair. It was a decision that I made and kept to for the remainder of my life. My relationship with Tommy never regained its old intimacy as his father's death was constantly there between us.

My job was unremitting but I was happy with my salary and the company rewarded my diligence which helped to support the three of us comfortably. In my free time I continued to help Father with the garden doing the jobs that he now found difficult. Extended family, work colleagues and villagers all shared the surplus produce. Life for me was becoming much easier and less emotional.

One day the following year whilst at the office, I received an unexpected telephone call from St Mary's School. Roger had contracted pneumonia and was in a critical condition. I found this news completely shocking. Roger had seemed well, apart from a little cough, when I had seen him on the previous Sunday.

My boss very kindly volunteered to drive me to the hospital and promised to inform my family of the situation. The journey from London to Margate was long and arduous and seemed to take forever. I just kept silently repeating to myself, 'Roger can't be seriously ill, it's impossible'.

On my arrival I was ushered into a small room where my son was lying in an Iron Lung. I rushed up to the grey cylinder. It was so noisy. Roger's entire body, other than his head, was encased within it. Stroking his cold forehead I realised he was unconscious. I turned to the doctor to voice my concerns when he said, "Mrs Barratt, sit down. I will open the ventilator and give you some time with your child."

I sat down beside Roger and cradled his body against my chest in a warm fluffy blanket, wanting to comfort and reassure him. With one little sigh he passed away.

I really found it difficult to remember the next few hours. Somebody took me home. I went to bed and took the tablet the doctor had given me to help me sleep but my night's sleep was very disturbed. I drifted in and out of consciousness wanting so much to wake from this nightmare. My darling Roger couldn't be dead. He was only twelve. In my dream he was still alive. I had seen him running and laughing, holding a bunch of dandelions for me as I sat on the lovely blanket that I had wrapped him in when I gave him his last cuddle.

I awoke to the harsh reality. I didn't know what I believed in. If there was a heaven perhaps Thomas would be waiting to care for our son and that love would earn his redemption. I needed so much to believe this. My heart and life seemed broken.

The irksome weeks, then months of anguish, laboured seamlessly one into another. Father and Thomas needed me to get on with my life. Poor Father felt guilty at living to his advanced years. I realised that both he and my surviving son were feeling their own pain but had tried to conceal their feelings to protect me. Knowing this jolted me back into the reality of having to cope with the everyday ups and downs of life.

Eleven

Prime Minister Neville Chamberlin had met with Adolf Hitler several times trying to broker a peaceful solution to avert another world war. Hitler however, wouldn't accept the peace plans and he refused to sign the declaration. When Germany invaded Poland Chamberlain was forced to declare war. It was 3 September 1939. Some people heard the news directly from the wireless, while others ran from house to house relating the news, as many didn't possess a wireless set. Supposition was now a fact. We were at war with Germany once again.

There was a mass evacuation of children from London. Many thousands were packed into trains with labels tied or pinned onto their coats saying who they were. Nobody knew where they were bound. Parents entrusted their children to the London authorities. We were so fortunate to live in Kent away from the city of London and the docks.

People dug bunkers and erected iron shelters in their

back gardens. Neighbour helped neighbour. Lawns were uprooted to make way for vegetables whilst the discarded turves were re-laid on the top of the shelters in the hope that German pilots would mistake them for parks and re-route their deadly cargo, should they ever bomb England. Life became very different. Everyone was full of apprehension not knowing what would happen should we be invaded. Not a soul believed that was a possibility; after all we were an island. Time passed by with this false sense of security.

Many felt aggrieved when the government removed all the iron railings and gates as they were needed to manufacture more guns and tanks. I felt ashamed of many peoples' selfish attitude. They were worrying about their gardens being exposed to trespassers but in the scheme of things this was a minor concern.

On 10th May 1940 Winston Churchill became Prime Minister. Later that month we received the shocking news about the evacuation of Dunkirk. The German forces had trapped the British and their Allies in an area along the northern coast of France. Small boats were commandeered to cross the channel to help bring the stranded troops home from the beaches and harbour of Dunkirk. In Kent, we watched the streams and estuaries fill with an unlikely flotilla of trawlers, tugs, fishing sloops, lifeboats and pleasure craft. It would seem that any craft that floated was used. We were staggered by the enormity of the rescue mission. Over six hundred craft managed to save more than three hundred thousand lives. Dunkirk showed us all that the war wasn't in some distant land but on our very own doorstep.

Soon to follow, in September that year, was the heavy bombing of the docks and the East End of London. Many other British cities were also targeted. The raids were carried out at night as opposed to the day time. This was to enhance the fear factor and was Hitler's attempt to destroy Britain's morale. The suffering was indescribable and many thousands were killed. The lucky ones kept their lives but lost their homes. By May 1942, 1.4 million people across the country had been made homeless. It had the effect of making me feel ashamed that I still went to bed in clean sheets and got up for breakfast as usual. Anxiety gripped our household as there were so many things to worry about.

Getting to work was a challenge, as daily routines changed by the hour due to unforeseen circumstances. Everyone tried to do their best to help each other in any way that they could. Father kept planting allotments for the women whose husbands were away or widows and old people he knew. In fact, anyone in need. He gathered all the plant seeds from everyone's allotments and gardens and stored them in the dark in air tight tins, in order to have continuity for the following year. We all shared everything as did most others. Should anybody be in need, someone somewhere, would have it or find it. For others, the 'black market' was eventually their response to rationing.

The black market was illegal and there were hefty

fines of up to £500 or two years imprisonment for those who were caught. Food for the black market often came from farms. In towns and cities, the black out assisted those who obtained their illicit goods. Most goods were purloined by breaking into warehouses or the docks.

I did my little bit for the war effort by knitting for the forces. I also gathered goods and made up parcels, as well as selling war bonds to anyone that could spare a pound or two. It was everybody's job to support our much-loved country. A great spirit of determination prevailed throughout Britain, often helped by the popular music of the time. Vera Lynn wasn't just the 'Forces Sweetheart,' her songs, 'We'll Meet Again' and 'There'll Always Be an England' were sung with sentiment wherever a crowd gathered.

Thomas had left school at sixteen with a Higher School Certificate. He had studied hard and it certainly paid off, as he now worked in an accountant's office. His dream was to be an accountant and own a partnership but this ambition slowly faded by the day. It was the same for everybody. Nobody expected life to be easy. Many highly qualified young men had been called up, therefore many companies were struggling to find staff. A lot of articles and apprenticeships were put on hold for the period of the war. We were fortunate as so many others had lost everything held dear to them. It did us good to talk to each other at the end of each day as we were able to share our fears and concerns.

Life continued in its austere fashion. As the war

progressed shortages abounded. First of all petrol was controlled, then basic food stuffs were rationed along with other commodities like clothing. Ration books were issued to everyone. Mothers of families did marvels with the little food allocated to each person. We did not starve as so many people did in the occupied countries. Mom and Pop Barratt managed to get the occasional parcel to us, sometimes through the kindness of their friends' sons who came to England as members of the Canadian Forces. Rationing continued after the war had ended in 1945. Sugar rationing didn't end until September 1953 and meat continued to be rationed for a further ten months after that.

I remember well one particular evening at the beginning of 1940. Both Father and I looked up to greet Thomas, as usual, when he returned home from work. His face was stern and unsmiling and he had a look of dogged determination about him.

As soon as he walked through the door he announced, "I've enlisted with the Canadian Air Force."

Both Father and I were speechless. Apparently as Thomas had joint nationality he could choose which country he wished to serve with. Had he waited for the usual call-up papers he wouldn't have had a choice. Naturally, he chose Canada. Only one thought whizzed around in my head and that was, that history was repeating itself. The only difference was that Thomas senior had served in the army. Two weeks later Thomas was off to join the British Commonwealth Air Training

Plan. He was nineteen and life for him as a young man in our home was never resumed again.

We had no choice but to wake up every morning and start each day afresh. Father's general well being always astounded me. I would give him covert looks to assess his health. He appeared reasonably well to me. Maybe it was the job he did, always in the open air, using all his muscles. Mentally he didn't allow his mind to get blocked with unnecessary worries, sleep never eluded him. If only I could be the same. The only thing that changed for Father was that he ceased to cycle when he reached seventy. The bicycle was relegated to the potting shed without one word being said. Another thing that amazed me about him was his aversion to taking tablets or drugs of any description. His healthy way of life was a good guide to follow.

If anyone had asked my father what his greatest achievement was he would no doubt have said, "I can't think of anything." But I do know that he was proud of being an unpaid advisor to the county council. He assessed soil and defined what soil conditions were suitable for certain crops. He also calculated how many crops could be grown per acre. I thought that it was an important job especially with all the food shortages that were present at that time.

Great Britain had to grow as much food as possible during the war. Merchant ships carrying food were always getting attacked by German U-Boats that would lay in waiting in packs. This was one of the prices we had to pay for being an island.

Travelling to work I noticed I was surrounded by many nationalities. There were many Americans, Polish and some called the Free French. Before long a greeting such as, ‘Hi Honey’ or ‘Cherie,’ became commonplace. These allies were all miles from home and I’m sure they were homesick too. Even though they carried the support of their various nations with them, I still gave them as many smiles as I could. I wanted to acknowledge that we too as a country were grateful for their support.

I missed Thomas greatly but like so many others I had to accept that he was doing his duty for King and Country. Evenings were the worst. I missed the chats after our meal when we used to share any amusing happenings of the day. Sometimes we would relate the tales to Father who would sigh and mutter, "I don’t know what the world is coming to."

My thoughts also often strayed to my lovely smiling Roger. Each year on his birthday in June I would wonder how much he might have grown or even if his abilities would have advanced with his years. I knew really they wouldn’t have. I don’t know why I did this because I always ended up shedding tears.

Joyce, my friend at work, invited me to stay with her one weekend. She lived in Stoke Poges. She thought a few days away from home would help me to gain peace and closure on the things that troubled my mind. Father was worried about me so he encouraged me to accept her invitation. It was four years since Roger had died and it dawned on me that I had not been away from my family since my return to England, just over ten years ago. It would be a complete change for me.

I knew Joyce attended church every Sunday and it was my intention to accompany her. We chose a weekend that suited us both. We spent Saturday afternoon shopping in Slough. It was such a tonic to me but we both enjoyed our day together. On Sunday morning we travelled by bus to Windsor to save time but it was quite a short journey and we could have easily walked the distance. I was surprised to find it was a Spiritualist church. I knew nothing of this faith. Joyce introduced me to her friends who were very welcoming and I became aware that everyone surrounding me was also gentle and calm. I would attend the church many more times, whenever I stayed at Stoke Poges. I always felt at peace after the service. Most religions believe in life after death but Spiritualism showed me that communication with deceased peoples' spirits could actually take place. I desperately wanted to communicate with Roger and believed it would be possible one day.

One Sunday I was aware of a man staring at me across the aisle. I had noticed him several weeks before. I felt a little uncomfortable and glanced around the church then back toward him. I found him doing the same and our eyes met briefly before we both quickly averted our gaze. I was later introduced to him by Joyce. His name was Henry Taylor. He was well over six feet tall with a moustache and short brown hair and was a musician in the Life Guard regiment. Henry came to church whenever he was able. He was obviously interested in spiritualism. We seemed attracted to each other which resulted eventually in our first date. I related all my circumstances to him and he did likewise. He loved his life in the army and was living alone at Combermere Barracks. We fell in love and life began again for me in every sense.

Father thought that he was a fine upstanding man and good enough for his widowed daughter. Thomas too was pleased for me. He was now stationed in South Africa with the Royal Canadian Air Force.

My relationship with Henry gradually deepened. We enjoyed each other's company and seemed at ease with one another. I realised just how serious our relationship had become when Henry invited me to meet his mother. There were many things to take in to account before arranging a date, mainly finding a time when Henry's leave coincided with his mother being free and me being able to take time off also Mrs Taylor wanted Henry to give me the grand tour of the house and the estate in private.

I carefully planned what I was going to wear. I searched my wardrobe for the smartest outfit I possessed. I was delighted at the prospect of meeting Henry's mother. Henry planned the journey in military style and told me I had to wear sensible shoes, as we would have to walk up a very long drive to the house.

In the end, the walk didn't materialise as Charles, the chauffeur, collected us from the end of the drive in the

Rolls Royce. It was a lovely surprise that Mrs Taylor had arranged. I felt like a movie star.

Henry's mother came down the steps to greet us. I liked her immediately as her first words to me were, "I think we ought to have a hug."

It was a simple gesture but bonded us instantly. We went on to enjoy a splendid lunch and chatted amiably for several hours until it was time to leave.

On the bus on the way home we each had so much to say. I felt very close to Henry. We cuddled and gave each other furtive kisses whenever the opportunity arose, such was our joy.

Over the months our love grew steadily and we were happy with our lives until the day I received some shocking news.

HENRY

1900 - 1940

Twelve

Green lawns rolled out of sight with a tree lined path which appeared to continue forever, like a never ending ribbon. For some unknown reason, I was never allowed to walk along it unaccompanied. At the end of this ribbon was a beautiful lake where ducks swam or waddled up a gentle slope into a little duck house that was in the centre. Beautiful, white, star shaped flowers with yellow centres and large round plate like leaves, floated on the surface of the water. It was enchanting. I learned later in life that these flowers were water lilies. Not only was the lake enchanting it was also mysterious, especially on misty days. My imagination used to run riot and I went on many boyhood adventures.

The lake was so vast it could be seen from all the upper rooms of the house. The house was built in the Neo-Renaissance style of a French château. It had many turrets which reminded me of the pictures I had seen in my childhood book of Grimm's Fairy Tales. In the few years that we lived there, I had never seen a single person walking the grounds besides several men who were the gardeners.

As I approached my fifth birthday a new word was introduced to me – school. This was a place that I had to attend and I wondered what it could be. I was anxious until my mama explained to me that it was a good place, and that I would like it because I would have other children to play with. Her words made me feel much better.

Our house was so big that I never saw other children, only 'grown up people' as I used to call adults. Sometimes I would catch a glimpse of them and they would smile at me but they lived in another part of our house. My mama didn't do housework as other women were employed for that undertaking. These women were very kind to me and would bring me chocolate. Sometimes they would give me my favourite sweet, a Sherbet Dab. Mama hated me being given this particular sweet because the yellow powder puffed out like dust. She was always concerned that the sherbet would fly onto the highly polished furniture leaving a sticky trail.

I fondly recall one occasion when Mama and I went out together on a special day trip. We caught a bus at the end of the drive. I liked that very much but the chauffeur had insisted that he drive us to the road. As a child I was impressed with the large, shiny, black car that had a silver lady flying on the front. I know now that she is called the Spirit of Ecstasy. We must have travelled in one of the first Rolls Royce motor cars with the new radiator mascot.

The bus pulled up in front of us when Mama raised

her hand. I wondered how the bus driver knew to stop when Mama waved to him. It was a memorable day. We visited shops where Mama made me try on lots of clothes before she purchased them. There were so many parcels that I had to help carry them. On our way home we stopped off at a large department store where I had the biggest ice cream, in the largest glass, that I had ever seen. The top was covered with cherries, a sprinkling of nuts and a fan wafer. It was the most wonderful day in my young life.

On arriving home, I changed my shoes and washed my hands ready for supper. We always ate together. Our meal was usually eaten in silence although we started by saying Grace and I always finished with thanking Mama and asking permission to leave the table. This day my mama asked me to stay where I was as she wanted to talk to me. I expected it to be something to do with school but it wasn't. She had already explained about that and I no longer felt scared at the thought of it. In fact, I was looking forward to school and sharing the experience with lots of other children.

Mama began by saying that now I was older I needed to know lots of things about our house. I learned that Ruscombe Hall wasn't our house. It belonged to a rich gentleman called Sir Richard Waters. Mama was the housekeeper and her job was to look after Sir Richard and his family, making sure that everything was in order for when he visited with his family and friends. The word rich didn't mean anything to me at that age. Nothing had changed as far as I was concerned, we would still allow them to share our house. How simple my life was when I was a child.

School started. My mama came with me every day for the first week. After that I was driven to the end of the drive by the chauffeur and his silver lady. It made me feel very grown up. I loved school and this feeling stayed with me for the rest of my days. I was happy with all my new friends. It is obvious to me now, that as a young child, I was very lonely. I didn't realise that I didn't live the life of a normal child. I behaved like an adult.

Days stretched into months and years. I did well in my Elementary School. Although I was not brilliant, I passed most tests at a reasonable level. I was in my eleventh year preparing for tests which if I passed would enable me to gain a place at the Higher Elementary School. If I achieved this, it would lead me to a better future.

These schools were for promising children aged 10 to 15. The curriculum included drawing, theoretical and practical science, a foreign language and elementary mathematics.

I took the exams in my stride. School was still the place I was most happy. In the summer of 1911, I found out I had passed. My mama gave me a present of a bicycle. I was beside myself with happiness. It opened up a new world as it gave me the freedom to explore new places by myself .

I rode all around the Ruscombe estate finding paths that I didn't know existed. After a while I was allowed to ride to school. My bicycle also enabled me to join the Scouts. I wasn't keen on football or cricket but I loved the public library and was always borrowing books. I discovered music and read avidly about the lives of various composers. The gift of a bicycle had made such a difference to my life.

At this time Mama decided that I was mature enough to be told the story of my papa's death. I had been told when I was younger that he had died. I thought that died meant that he had gone away. It hadn't caused me any trauma, as far as I was aware.

Now I was to hear something different. My mama rarely smiled and to me, as a child, she had always looked sad. I remember wondering why she worked in this huge house when it made her so unhappy. In my whole childhood I could never remember her going out or being invited to anybody's home. I knew I had grandparents, maybe even aunts and uncles but they were never mentioned. As a child I assumed that everybody lived the same way. Later my schooling certainly made me think differently about so many aspects of my life.

Mama began by saying, "You know your Papa was in the army?"

I didn't know until that moment, so that was my first piece of information.

She continued without drawing breath.

"You know that there was a war called the Boer War, don't you? It was fought in South Africa. Papa was a sergeant in the Essex Regiment and he was very well thought of by his fellow men. Anyhow, the Boer War was a terrible war. So many men were killed at the various battles. I hate the South Africans and their heathen country. I still have your Papa's watch and a purple, silk battle scarf. Your Papa was so proud when his brother sergeants presented him with his silver pocket watch. It is inscribed upon the back with their sentiments. The names of all the battles fought in South Africa are listed on that scarf. They will be yours when you are older."

She then continued more calmly.

"Papa and I were so happy when we discovered that I was expecting you. We talked of our future and made lots of plans for the years ahead. These dreams collapsed when your papa was killed at the battle of Driefontein in March 1900. I was five months pregnant and my worst nightmare had come true.

As well as my loss, I was without money and unable to work. My parents supported me until my small pension arrived and you were born. Your birth Henry, inspired me to sort out my future. I concluded that any job I took would have to include board and lodgings, one which also included you. It was very difficult. Several times I moved into a job, only to have to move again as people changed their minds. A baby crying needing attention wasn't acceptable to them. I was always looking out for my next job. I found this position when you were nearly three years old. Sir Richard and Lady Walters have appreciated me and over the years have been very considerate of your welfare too."

It was so much to take in. So many unspoken questions had been answered. It was clear to me why my mama seldom laughed or smiled. It was such a tragic story and though I was young I could feel her pain. I couldn't feel hurt for my papa as I had never known him. I burst into tears for my mama and her hard life. For the first time that I recalled, she smiled and opened her arms, which I ran into. It was the first cuddle she had given me that I was aware of. It was to become the first of many. I looked up into her smiling face, tears were streaming down her cheeks but the beautiful smile told me that she knew for the first time in years that she loved and was loved in return.

With all these revelations life changed for me. I felt more valued. I now understood and appreciated so many unexplained actions by my mama. Life had been so difficult for her. It was my hope that she now wouldn't feel so lonely. From then on we shared little smiles without needing a reason. Every day we became a little closer, talking about anything that came into our minds. We cherished every moment that we were in each other's company.

I took advantage of the fact that Mama now informed me about Sir Richard's forthcoming visits. This enabled me to wander all around the house when the family were absent. It was such a privilege.

I was able to look at renowned paintings, exquisitely carved furniture, fine porcelain and all the wonderful treasures collected by the Walters' ancestors. I would run my fingers over the keys of the piano in the Blue Drawing Room. Various other instruments were kept in their cases but I didn't dare handle these. Every spare moment I had I spent exploring and investigating the house. There were rules I had to obey. I wasn't to lift up anything, touch any polished surfaces or open any cabinets and drawers. I was glad that Mama hadn't realised that I may have already done so, in innocence. The grand staircase was my special pretend space. I would walk down it casually imagining that I was Sir Richard. I perfected my gentleman's walk. On one occasion bursts of laughter made me jump. Mama was hiding on the top gallery with her housemaids watching my every move, listening to my conversation with myself as Sir Richard.

This staircase was to figure largely in my future. I descended it on this particular day to hear music coming from the Blue Drawing Room. I thought that Mama was playing a trick, pretending to be a ghost in the drawing room by playing the phonograph. I rushed through the door to find it was Sir Richard playing the violin. Mama had forgotten to remind me that he was visiting. Sir Richard didn't stop playing but mouthed to me to sit down until he had finished the piece. I was really frightened at being found there but at the same time, I was spellbound at his playing.

On finishing, Sir Richard rang for Mama. I felt fearful. The same feeling was reflected in her eyes when she saw me sitting on the chair. Sir Richard requested a tray of tea with biscuits then added, "It's all right, don't worry Mrs

Taylor. I intend to have a few words with Thomas."

Mama left us and we didn't have to wait too long before William, one of the footmen, brought in the tray of tea. After we had finished Sir Richard asked me how I came to be in that part of the house. With the innocence of the young I told him the truth, that I loved the paintings and the carved furniture.

"What did you think of my playing?"

I hung my head not knowing what to answer.

"Was I any good?" he probed.

"Oh yes," I quickly retorted, "I really mean, very good."

"Would you like to learn a musical instrument?"

"Yes I would."

The answer shot from my mouth with such haste I felt like a ventriloquist's dummy.

"I will speak to your mother."

Within a week violin lessons were arranged with a local teacher.

A parcel arrived at the house addressed to me. A beautiful old violin in its padded case was inside. It came from a special place in London. On seeing it, my mama said, "It doesn't matter that it is second-hand."

"I don't care, I like it."

At eleven I had no idea of its real worth but years later I discovered it was a Charles Boullangier violin. This explained my music teacher's reaction when she first saw it. She was very impressed by the violin and told me that she would give every penny she earned to own it.

What a fortunate boy I was. A bicycle had been the

catalyst for the first change in my life and now there was a second opportunity, in the form of a beautiful second-hand violin.

I made steady progress with my violin lessons. Practising was no chore to me as I loved every moment. When the Waters family were away I was allowed to practise in the drawing room. Life was sheer bliss.

Mama told me that she wanted to discuss a proposition with me. I realised that it had to be something serious as we discussed most things informally every day. It turned out to be very serious. Later that day she suggested that with my interest in music and my family connections with the army, I might like to apply for a place in the Military School. If successful I could start in the term of my fourteenth birthday. The Military School would teach me to play many more instruments, as well as following the usual curriculum. At the same time I would receive board and lodgings and military training. It was a lot to absorb but I wasn't daunted at the prospect. To learn to play percussion instruments was my dream. Mama said she would communicate with the school to see if I was eligible.

By the time all the paperwork was received the idea of me leaving home saddened her. Selfishly, I was still eager at the prospect of my exciting future. Life was like a jigsaw puzzle and I hoped all the parts would eventually fit together. Fourteen was the usual age to start work for working class children as it enabled them to help support their families. Mama didn't want this for me and she concentrated all her efforts to secure a better future for me.

My belief that it was just a matter of filling in a few forms before I packed my bag, turned out to be unrealistic. A great many forms had to be filled in and then returned. My biggest asset to my acceptance was my papa and my grandfather having served in the army. Everything written and submitted had to be correlated. It took such an age that I began to wonder if I would ever receive a positive reply.

Several months went by without news from the school, and then a letter arrived. Mama must have been impatient for me to arrive home to open it. I recall the vision she made running from the house, waving an envelope in her hand. I wobbled on my bicycle, nearly over balancing in my effort to wave back. I was thrilled that my mama had waited for me to open it. She handed it to me saying,

"This is my first acknowledgement of you as a young man."

I felt ten feet tall, valued and respected. I wanted to cry but thank goodness I didn't, as it would have spoilt my new image. We were both impatient to read the contents. Mama sat on the stone steps which lead up to the house. That was the first occasion she had done so and it would be the last. I sat next to her and made as though to rip the envelope open. Mama took it from me and opened it efficiently with a paper knife before handing it back. I removed the letter. Its first words were, *'We are pleased...'* I got no further than that when I had to make a dash for the bathroom.

Although it was an offer of entry it was subject to a strict medical examination. It appeared so laborious. Each stage seemed to take weeks.

As it cost so much money to train entrants, the school had to make sure that the applicants were applying for the right reason, with an intention to study and accept the discipline. In my heart I intended to do both. It was a great day when my acceptance was cleared. I was now Boy H. Taylor of the Earl of Runcton's Military School, Crookham. I was to start in fourteen days. When the time came to pack it only took a few minutes to fill my case. Even the suitcase had to conform to regulations in both colour and size as decreed by the military school. I was allowed one change of clothing plus my musical instrument. Suddenly everything became a reality. It was time for farewells to the life I had known it. The goodbye could no longer be deferred. I had well and truly grown up.

Sir Richard was at home and came to say farewell. He shook my hand and said, "Good luck Boy Taylor." As a retired colonel he knew the correct terminology. I felt impressed and reassured.

Mama travelled with me to Crookham. Sir Richard allowed his chauffeur Charles to drive us, instructing him to deliver us a little way from the school. He laughed as he said, "It wouldn't do for Boy Taylor to arrive in a Rolls Royce."

It would have made me an object of ridicule from the

older boys. He was right. New boys do suffer when starting new boarding schools. I was no exception.

Thirteen

The military school proved to be a hard and disciplined way of life but my love of music carried me along. There were exams every three months in both general education and music. No one was allowed to move up a class until they had passed. Should you fail several times your parents would be requested to remove you from the school. This didn't happen often as the fear of that disgrace intensified your desire to get a first grade pass.

My first new instrument was the drums. I was ecstatic. As soon as you were proficient you were allowed to participate in the early morning parades. I felt nothing in life could be as superb. I was always on the drill ground first as I couldn't wait for the parade to start. In general, as a musician, life at school wasn't so bad. You spent hours learning about music and how to play your chosen instrument, then hours upon hours practising. All of which gave me great pleasure. I was so lucky that Sir Richard had given me my first start in music and that my papa's career had enabled the military school to accept me. Looking back I realised that my mama had had both the strength and tenacity to encourage me towards a career which would in turn lead to a better future. I was grateful to each of them.

I was proficient at playing the violin and now the drums. The musical director was the officer who decided if your standard merited learning a new instrument. Each new instrument, plus the ones you had moved on from, required daily practice. The teacher didn't want to know how you would accomplish this, only the fact that you had. It certainly was a punishing schedule. At the time, I did not realise that this was when you were assessed on your capabilities. The assessor only wanted to know your strengths, not weaknesses. I could not say that there was never a time when I wanted to give up, as there were many such occasions.

I started school in 1914 at the outbreak of the First World War. We were fortunate that we were too young to be serving on the front line along side thousands of other young men. Our lives were barely affected by the horrors of war.

After several years of working hard we were allowed to venture in to Portsmouth on our weekly afternoons off. We would look around the shops, buying any essentials that we needed, then we would seek the local pubs for a beer or two. The locals knew all about the Boys from the Military, as they used to call us. Most of us had an eye for the girls. Many of my school friends had a 'love them and leave them' attitude. I was ashamed of our Jack the Lad attitudes, respect for these girls was not that apparent. In the main most of us had had the upbringing which labelled girls that frequented ale houses as 'no better than they should be.' After a couple of drinks I would leave my friends and walk along the quay towards the docks. It was a restricted zone to all civilians but not for us. Although we were in uniform we had to still go through check points and provide a form of identity.

I used to watch the big merchant ships alongside the battle ships, some of which would have brought food to feed the nation. All the battle ships were camouflaged in grey. Heavy guns stood on their upper decks and I used to stare in awe, wondering how these colossal boats stayed afloat with all that heavy weight. It fascinated and yet distressed me to see their upper structures riddled with holes. The ships had obviously seen a lot of action. The marks of war were evident for all to see. I walked away feeling somewhat guilty. How could we be laughing, joking and drinking beer when our brothers in arms were suffering? I hoped that the rumours circulating school were correct and that the war was almost at its end. I then thought about the concerts that we gave to promote money for the boys in Saxe blue and hoped it really did help both them and their families. It was a small drop of water in a large ocean.

It was time for me to move on to another new instrument. It was the trumpet. It gave me such a feeling of excitement. I practised with such zeal. My ambition was to play reveille. I couldn't wait for each day to arrive.

I rose earlier than usual to practise both the violin and the drums, what a contrast of sounds. Our practice hall was vast and was soundproofed, even so the sound echoed around. I think I remained in raptures for months. It was as though I was on some kind of drug. I became addicted to the trumpet. In any spare time, even as short a period as fifteen minutes, I would race across to the far side of the playing fields to practise my trumpet. I took a lot of ribbing from my fellow pupils, all of whom thought I was crazy. Our musical director knew that I did this and said he didn't object, as long as I didn't play reveille. Years later I was told what the colonel had said of me,

"That boy doesn't play the trumpet. He is the trumpet."

To a musician that was the ultimate praise.

Mama became used to me being away. I'm sure she missed my company but she never complained. I didn't have the burden of worrying about how she managed because I knew there were others at Ruscombe Hall who would keep an eye on her. My mama informed me that Sir Richard always enquired about my welfare. He now worked for the war office. Lots of people were staying at the house and more staff was taken on to help. Mama's responsibility increased, so she never had time to be lonely. We remained very close and when I was home on leave, I would regale her with tales of Earl Runcton's. How different the relationship between us was. It was always a joy to see her and regret when I had to leave, every moment counted.

One of the school's activities was to entertain retired

soldiers. Army vehicles would collect them and bring them to our vast dining hall. They were fed by the school cooks and then given a concert. Various school bands played all the old tunes of the day such as the Colonel Bogey March, The Ragtime Soldier Man and It's A Long Way To Tipperary. The concert always ended with an uplifting sing-along and I enjoyed these occasions. After playing we would go amongst the ex-servicemen and talk to them. It was usual for them to enjoy reminiscing about days gone by. Most of these veterans were in their seventies and eighties and some had even fought in the Crimean War.

I introduced myself to a couple of them, one of whom said, "I knew a Sergeant Taylor but he was in the Essex regiment."

I was eager to find out more. Everything he said about my papa was accurate. He even knew that my papa was shot and died at Driefontein in the second Boer War. There was no uncertainty in his recall and knowledge. I worked out the old soldier's age and it married with everything I had been told about Papa. I intended to confirm it by looking up this corporal's army records, as soon as the first opportunity arose.

There were two Boer Wars, which took place in South Africa. The first was from 1880 to 1881and the second from 1899 to 1902. The British Empire fought against the Dutch settlers of two independent Boer republics, the Orange Free State and the Transvaal Republic. The battle of Driefontein in 1900 was the last attempt to prevent the

British from occupying Bloemfontein, the capital of the Orange Free State. The Boers organised a defensive line and fought well even though they were outnumbered. The British lost 82 men and hundreds more were wounded. Boer losses were estimated at 102 dead and 22 taken prisoner. The British captured Bloemfontein three days later and they thought the war would soon be won.

I couldn't sleep that night with the excitement of this discovery. Corporal Anderson was the only person that I had met, who had known my papa, other than my mama. I didn't know whether to tell her. She was nicely settled into the life she had made for herself. What would be gained from the revelation? I concluded there was no rush and that I would tell her after I had had another talk with the Corporal. A date was set for me to visit him on my next day off. I couldn't wait. The days wouldn't pass swiftly enough.

There was no problem finding the home where Corporal Anderson now lived. It was a short journey from Crookham. Matron opened the door and I was invited in. I explained that I had come to see Fred Anderson.

"I am so sorry to inform you of this, but Fred passed away two days ago. What a shock for you. Did you know him well?"

"No. We had only just met. But I was hoping to get to know him. He knew my papa."

I was shattered and left the home feeling completely numb.

Apparently, he too had been thrilled and had told his

various friends at the nursing home about our meeting. Matron had found him asleep in bed that morning. However, it was the sleep from which you never awake. I just couldn't believe it. I was so thankful that I hadn't related the story to my mama.

I was startled by the impact this gentleman's death had upon me. I had always felt that my papa was a remote figure in my life but I was now beginning to feel that this wasn't so anymore. My affection for him had been lying dormant. The joy of talking to somebody who had actually known him had opened my heart. The image of my papa had grown more substantial. I surmised that had my papa survived there might have been a possibility that I would have had brothers and sisters. I knew I would have to talk to Mama. I wanted to know everything that she could remember about him. I always thought she must have loved him dearly as she had never considered marrying again. Being widowed at such a young age with a baby, must have been so difficult. If she had acquired a new husband she would have solved many of her problems. I looked forward in anticipation to my next visit home.

It turned out that Mama wasn't able to relate much more than I already knew. She decided however that as I was approaching the end of my school years, it was the appropriate time to present me with my papa's medals, watch and battle scarf. These meant so much more to me then than they would have done had I been younger. I read the inscription on the back of the watch from his brother sergeants at the Institute of Musketry. Papa had been presented with this souvenir in January 1878. I suddenly realised he had served in the army for over twenty years and I felt closer to him. These precious tributes gifted to my papa then handed down to me remained with me all my life.

It was the perfect time to tell Mama that I had decided to make the army my future career and that I had applied to the Household Cavalry Regiment.

Two months later I received a letter informing me that I had been accepted into the Life Guards, having successfully passed my medical and my previous interviews. I was jubilant and decided to celebrate with other 'Earlies,' as we military boys were nick named.

A few of us decided to join our friends who had found a quaint local pub. It didn't matter that we were in our civilian clothing as everybody knew we were from Earl Runcton's by our haircuts. Everyone at The Boar's Head also knew that we didn't cause trouble with the local lads. Black eyes or cut faces would have resulted in us being put on a charge and fear of that kept us well behaved, by and large. I wanted to make the most of my time left with my close mates. I would soon be leaving for my new post and life would never be the same.

During the evening I noticed one of the bar maids who continuously smiled when she was serving. My brain worked over time. How could I grab her attention? I offered to get the boys' refills. Each time she served me I chatted with her.

She looked around 5 feet 6 inches tall, was very slender with long platinum blonde hair and she had the deepest of blue eyes. I thought she was beautiful. In short, I was smitten. At the end of the evening I called goodbye to her as we left. She replied, "I'll look forward to seeing you again." I was determined to return on my own the following week.

Days dragged by. All I could think of was my next visit to the Boar's Head and that smile. I confided in the boys that I liked Sarah, the bar maid, and they were pleased for me. I was apprehensive about the whole thing. I was still a virgin and I knew I would be petrified of any relationship that progressed beyond a kiss. Girls always think that it's only the female sex that is scared about the intimacies of life. That is not true. Boys are just as petrified, the only difference is we don't admit it.

For weeks my free time was spent visiting the Boar's Head. Sarah arranged her time off to coincide with my visits. Her work entitled her to board and lodging but her bedroom was out of bounds. Sarah soon found a way that enabled us to spend private time together. The use of the fire escape solved our problems. On the first occasion that we made love, I left on winged feet. I smiled all the way back to Crookham. I didn't speak with anyone on the way home as I didn't want to spoil how I was feeling. I was in a state of euphoria.

I tried to slip back into school without awakening anybody but as soon as I slid into my bed the whole dormitory sat up and cheered. I was harangued with questions.

"How was it then Taylor?"

"Come on Harry, tell all."

"Did you need any help?"

I yelled back at them, "Sod off. Not a chance!" and covered my head with a pillow.

Within a few months everything changed. Sarah informed me she was pregnant. I was horrified as I only liked her. It certainly was not a love affair. I couldn't think of how I was going to tell Mama. I knew there was only one thing I could do and that was to marry the girl.

I could see my whole life crumbling before me. How selfish I was. Sarah had to break the news to her parents whilst my task was to tell my mama that I was getting married and the reason why. I dreaded the thought. Five minutes of pleasure had changed the course of our lives.

Fourteen

There were only four guests at the wedding, Mama, Sarah's parents, and my Best Man. It was a quiet, sombre affair at the Portsmouth Register Office. There were no smiles of joyfulness only the two families shaking hands. After the ceremony I returned to Earl Runcton's and Sarah went home with her parents. It wasn't the best of beginnings.

I sat on my bed at school reflecting on the enormity of what had happened. I had been a bloody idiot. Here I was not quite eighteen and a married man with a child on the way. What had I done? Two lives had been ruined. Why hadn't I sort advice from the Chaplin or my Headmaster? I felt as though I was a boy again waiting for someone to remedy my mistakes. It was at that moment that the truth revealed itself to me. No one had made me do anything I didn't want to do. I now had responsibilities and it was up to me alone to deal with them. I would have to begin by talking with Sarah. I had been utterly selfish in only thinking of the consequences for me and my career.

As soon as I could I met with Sarah at her parents' home. We were left alone and were therefore able to discuss our fears and plans for the future. Staying apart would have been the easy option but we needed to consider the baby. Both of us felt that we had to give our marriage a chance. Maybe we could be happy as a family. I left Sarah and her parents feeling much more positive. A more mature version of me walked away from Sarah's family home that evening. I felt I was in control again.

My first task was to request family quarters at my new posting. Nothing could proceed until this was finalised. Until such time, Sarah would remain at her parents with me visiting whenever I was able. Sarah had accepted that her future would be much more constrained than previously. I had grown up in households that had been run like military establishments, going to Earl Runcton's Military School had only been an extension of that life. For Sarah it would mean observing rules to comply with living in married quarters. I felt sure that she would take it all in her stride. We would be living in Windsor and there would be plenty of places for us to explore.

I was reluctant to leave some of the Earlies, as most of my friends had been with me from my first day. A few had also applied to serve with the Household Cavalry and were still waiting to hear if they had been accepted. I assumed that my papa's army career had assisted me once again.

Life became hectic. I found it hard to believe that I

had accumulated so much clutter in my time at Earl Runcton's. Why we keep old exam papers, cards, old magazines etc is puzzling. I resolved never to repeat this mistake. Needless to say I did, many more times in my life.

In my efforts to be prepared for this move, I hadn't taken into account that the moving of my instruments would be the biggest challenge. Although many of them belonged to Earl Runcton's I had managed to buy my own drums and trumpet. These with my beloved violin needed specialised packing. Moving day finally arrived and it wasn't the ordeal that I had expected it to be. The carriers did a superb job.

Life at Earl Runcton's Military School was over. I now resided in Windsor at Combermere Barracks, one mile from Windsor Castle. The barracks date back to 1804 and since then they had always been the quarters of the Household Cavalry Regiment. I was to be accommodated in the married quarters but had to wait my turn and I was told it could take several months. Sarah was disappointed as like me, she thought she would be joining me in a few weeks.

Music continued to occupy the largest part of my life. Horse riding became second nature to me after I had completed my twelve week riding course. I was put in charge of my own horse named Valour. He stood at well over 16 hands and was a five year old black gelding with three white legs and a blaze of white running from his forehead to his nose. These horses were known as

'Cavalry Blacks' and they went through a year's intensive schooling preparing them for a life of parades as well as getting them accustomed to vast crowds, traffic and noise.

Even when I was physically exhausted from the hours of music practice, I still had to polish brasses and wax the leather of saddle, tack and boots. This could take up to three hours. I used to take particular pride in waxing my jackboots. They were waxed hard and had many layers of polish applied so that they shone like burnished jet. The finish of our boots was often the source of fierce competition amongst us.

I enjoyed 'watering orders.' This was the time I spent each morning exercising my beautiful horse in the park. I used to speak to him as we rode, horses are so intuitive. I found it easier to talk to Valour than I did to my fellow guards. I would tell him all my problems and when dismounting I would always kiss his neck, give him a mint and say thank you. After a while when we had both got to know each other well, I would tease him and walk off without giving him his rewards. This would bring a snorting from his nostrils followed by a neigh which he would continue until I walked back and completed the ritual.

Sarah was keeping well and seemed to be accepting of the wait and happy with our relationship. Mama frequently wrote to her at her parents' house. She also sent parcels of baby clothes that she had knitted. Goodwill abounded from both sides of the family.

Upon my return one morning after 'watering orders,' I was handed a letter by the farrier. It was from Sarah's father. He said I should come to Hampshire as quickly as possible because Sarah had gone into labour. I was terrified. I knew nothing about babies being born. Even the word labour didn't convey its meaning to me. I was so ignorant in these matters. I couldn't just leave everything and go as army protocol had to be observed. Eventually permission from the right quarters was given and I was able to leave Windsor and set off to Portsmouth.

I arrived at Sarah's parents' home tired and in a state of panic. I banged on the door so hard that my father- in-law shouted loudly, "Hold your horses. I'm coming."

We were both very agitated. Sarah's mother was dashing in and out of the kitchen with one arm laden with towels and in the other she carried a hot steaming bucket of water. She was so absorbed that I didn't receive any greeting. A midwife called down the stairs, "Don't worry. All is going to plan. Sarah is a strong girl."

I remember thinking, in my ignorance, why do women have to be strong to have a baby? After all, it is a natural process. I learned much more as I got older. We sat for several hours and consumed many cups of tea. Suddenly the miraculous yell of a baby reached our ears. Sarah's father jumped up and shook my hand in congratulations. My mother- in -law called down the stair well, "You have a son and both Sarah and he are well."

I was surprised to feel such a strong emotion welling up within me and my eyes were brimming with tears. I rushed upstairs to see them both. Sarah looked tired but very pretty as she sat up in bed. Her face was radiant and she gave me such a special smile as she cradled the baby in her arms. I looked down at my son hardly believing that I had been a part of making this little child.

We discussed naming him. I did not have strong feelings about names, whatever Sarah chose would be fine with me. Her choice was to name him after her grandfather, Samuel.

Sarah was confined to bed for two weeks with baby Samuel in his crib at her side. We were still waiting for married quarters and appeared to be way down the list. I continued to work as hard as possible. Every moment was occupied with the demands of the regiment. Being a Life Guard had many different pressures with ceremonial parades and state occasions which included escorting the royal family. It was a wonderful privilege. Many of the rehearsals were practised late at night or in the early hours of the morning. It made it so much easier without the traffic and members of the public around.

On 11 November 1918 at Compiègne in France, the armistice was signed between the allies of World War I and Germany for the cessation of hostilities on the Western Front. I had been so fortunate to escape the horror of fighting in the trenches. I was eighteen and I received my orders one month later, in the December, for my new posting. I was to be sent as part of the Expeditionary Force to Europe, which meant I would miss Samuel's first Christmas. During my sixty two day tour of France I witnessed sights that are too abhorrent to recall and my fervent wish was for Samuel never to experience the same.

The following July I was given leave. The days passed by so quickly. My mind was always in a state of rehearsal, awaiting the next military event. Being married with a child was not the best of situations. Army life was uppermost in my thoughts both day and night. There was little room for the normal responsibilities of marriage, especially at such a distance. Sarah and Samuel were still living with Sarah's parents on the outskirts of Portsmouth.

In my heart I knew that I didn't feel the passion for Sarah that I felt for music and the army. Each visit to see her and the baby became harder for us both. The anxiety of desperately wanting to hear about us moving in to married quarters dwindled by the day. I knew the fault was mine.

On my visits we would take the baby in his pram for walks in the park but it was all so false, our relationship had become that of two good friends. Sarah was a better person than me and suggested we should be honest with each other and admit that our marriage was a mockery. I wish that I could declare that I was shocked but it would be untrue. I was relieved.

We arranged that I would visit as often as I could and still support them financially. We also agreed to inform our own parents about the situation between us. Mama and Sarah's parents were not in the least surprised and the fact that we were not going to seek a divorce seemed to please them.

I remained in my bachelor apartment for years as I rose through the ranks. The regiment had so many marvellous occasions to prepare for and to dress in our ceremonial uniforms always felt an honour. We all pre-inspected each other before mounting our horses to verify that all was as it should be before our officers gave us the final once over. Our horses seemed to share the same pride. They actually performed best when they were on public parades. It was only when they saw their troopers in full dress regalia that this special behaviour occurred.

I continued to visit Sarah and my son whenever I could. Neither Sarah nor I showed any interest in other partners and we still remained legally married. Divorce was never discussed by either of us or our parents.

Samuel left school in 1933 at the age of fifteen. I had tried to encourage him with music but he was not a bit interested and as for the army he thought it was an appalling life.

I hadn't been a good role model to him in either of these things. It saddened me a little but in fairness to Samuel, I hadn't been a shining example to follow. Sarah had told me that he was always drawing and loved art. I really knew so little of my son's achievements or ambitions. I had grown up without a father but I had always known that he had died in battle. It was hard for me to admit but my poor son had been abandoned by me to some degree. How could I expect him to love and respect me? I knew that my papa had had no choice but I did have one and I chose the army over my family. This decision haunted me forever.

Sarah was both a good mother and daughter. She decided to continue her career by training as a chef in the same inn that had employed her as a barmaid. These skills supported her for her entire life. We remained good friends, and we both tried to make our son Samuel our first priority.

Within the regiment, pressures never decreased. If anything, I found it more demanding as I advanced through the ranks. There were always new musical arrangements to be learned and then practised. My love of music never diminished and it enabled me to survive when the purpose of my life eluded me. I went through a period of self recrimination, feeling that I didn't deserve to be happy. It was Sarah who told me to move on and to do something different. She was an example to me and still obviously cared about the future of her son's father.

I was nearly at the end of my army career and the fact that we were now at war with Germany again made me feel wretched. The last war was meant to be the war to end all wars. I started reading again and one of the books I read was the Bible. I found it a remarkable and enlightening experience. I also found it comforting.

I decided to attend as many different churches as possible to find out if I could accept the Christian belief of the existence of heaven. I wanted to believe but was not convinced. I tried each church within walking distance of the barracks. I enjoyed their services and each one had made me welcome. Over the months, I had met so many kind and caring people but I still wasn't sure of what I believed in.

I was now at the end of my search. Only one church remained for me to investigate and that was the Spiritualist Church. I expected their service to be different from the others that I had attended and it was. From my first visit I felt different about myself but I couldn't explain how or why. I found the church a peaceful place and each person seemed to emit a calm and loving persona. I could relate to the principle in Spiritualism of the continuous existence of the human soul. I wanted the church to help me make contact with my papa. I made a commitment to return regularly when my leave permitted. Mama and several of my friends all said they had observed a change in me. I wanted to believe that this could be the start of a different way of thinking and a new path forward.

After the Sunday service I began to stay behind for refreshments and to chat to other people. I felt enriched by their interest in me. I knew that I would be able to return their kindness when the opportunity arose. Music would be my gift. I would be able to play for them whenever they wished.

One particular lady in the congregation always appeared to be glancing at me. One Sunday she stood beside me drinking coffee whilst talking to others. I was able to observe her without her knowing. She was short. I guessed her height was around 5 feet 2 inches because she was almost level with my shoulder. She had brown hair and I detected a slight accent which I couldn't put my finger on. My attraction to her was very strong. We were finally introduced to each other although she already knew my name and that I was a soldier. Her name was Esther.

We stood chatting totally absorbed with each other. She was a widow with one son and lived with her father. We didn't want to stop talking but virtually all our fellow worshippers had left and we felt obligated to follow.

"Will I see you next Sunday?"

"I hope so," she replied with a smile.

It was only a couple of weeks after meeting Esther that we shared our first date. I invited her to a meal followed by a visit to the cinema. We discovered we both liked Humphrey Bogart films and we enjoyed each other's company.

During the course of the evening I found out a little more about her. She lived with her father in West Farleigh, Kent. Esther was adamant that she didn't want to talk about being widowed but she did tell me that her husband Thomas had cheated on her and that the hurt of the betrayal had never left her. She went on to tell me her only son, Thomas, was serving with the Canadian Air Force and I wondered if this accounted for her accent. Joyce was her friend from work and she lived in Stoke Poges which explained why Esther, like me, could only attend the church spasmodically.

Within a few weeks she invited me to West Farleigh to meet her father. He was such a gentle man and I wasn't at all surprised to find out that he was a gardener. It complimented his attitude to life.

Mr B, as I eventually called him, made me very welcome. I knew he was concerned about Esther being alone. He confided in me, that up until now, Esther hadn't shown any interest in other men. In fact, I was the only man she had taken home. I felt so proud and honoured to hear this. It persuaded me to think of my future, hopefully with Esther.

It was now time for me to make a commitment. I asked Esther if she would consider living with me. It would enable us to see how our relationship would develop. I was both surprised and thrilled when she agreed. I knew I had to tell her about Sarah and my son Samuel but I decided to bide my time and wait until the right moment.

As I was still living in bachelor quarters it meant requesting a transfer to married accommodation. I didn't know how this would be received by the army especially as I only had a year or so left to serve.

ESTHER

1940 - 1948

Fifteen

I was pregnant at forty-one and I was not overjoyed. I was in a state of sheer disbelief. My erratic body had lied to me. I thought another pregnancy was impossible. I didn't tell Henry until a further month had passed, hoping I was wrong but at the same time thinking that he would be happy at having his first child. I chose my time to tell him of the news.

His loud, "No," reverberated around the walls of the room. "You can't be," he yelled. "I'm married."

For the second time in my life I fainted and hit the floor.

The weeks that followed were hellish and we had row after row with very long periods of silence in-between. Neither of us wished to initiate a resolution. I was both hurt and furious at the same time. I couldn't believe that Henry had deceived me. Why did he feel he couldn't have told me the truth? He knew I had already experienced despicable deceit from Thomas.

In the end we made an effort to discuss things civilly. Henry said that witnessing my distress supported his reason for keeping the truth from me. I wondered if I could ever truly forgive him.

Apparently, Henry's wife didn't believe in divorce even though she and Henry had been living apart for years. I felt there were so many decisions to be made in the short time available before the baby's birth. The biggest one being, should I live with Henry as I'd previously agreed? Could I ever trust him again? Perhaps I would be better off staying put at Willow Cottage until after the birth? In the end the decision was taken out of my hands.

I went into labour without any elation, only fear for the future. Nurses told me my labour was long due to my age. Our daughter was stillborn. My will to live left me and my condition deteriorated.

Henry never left my side. Thomas was given compassionate leave and was flown home from South Africa. My recovery was slow. Unknown to me, when Henry had found out I was pregnant, he had written to his wife Sarah explaining the situation and he had pleaded with her for a divorce. Sarah sent a letter agreeing but it arrived the day after our daughter was born. It felt like a consolation prize to me.

Somehow we survived this trauma and we married when the divorce was finalised. By then my health had improved a little. I moved out of Willow Cottage leaving its comfort but taking with me Father's love and so many memories.

Moving into the barracks with the constraints of army

life was hard to adjust to. There were so many rules and regulations to abide by. I felt my freedom had vanished into thin air and that I couldn't complain as we were at war. I was however, more than grateful that Henry was nearing the end of his service with the Life Guards and it was highly unlikely that he would be called to serve abroad. Fortunately, my old job had been kept open for my return.

My lovely colleagues understood and supported me whole heartedly in my time of need. Once more work was my salvation. During my times of great trouble it was a source of strength that I clung to.

On my arrival at work in the mornings I appeared to be a calm efficient woman, able to control both the staff and administration. However, inside I felt like a frightened woman who had lost her direction. I had to talk to myself and give encouragement just to get me through the day. I felt I had become two people but I needed them both to survive.

Life in the barracks was more difficult than I expected. As mature newcomers and recently bereaved, our young neighbours didn't know how to handle us or our situation. I just kept my head down and tried to be polite. I would pass the time of day with them on my way to and from work but that's as far as it went.

For me the army's strict security and accountability were difficult to tolerate but not so for Henry, who really couldn't understand why it bothered me. It had been this way the whole of his life and he had never enjoyed privacy even as a child. So we agreed to differ in our opinions on this matter. Nonetheless, it was only when we had moved in together that I began to understand how demanding his military life was.

Henry's life was one of rehearsals for concerts and ceremonial parades in addition to his normal duties. His splendid cuirass and Albert helmet had to be gleaming. His horse had hours spent on him too, plus saddles and jackboots always needed to be polished. It was awesome to see the Life Guards in all their splendour. Henry always stood out. The red plume on his helmet and his grey mount made him easy to spot. Being a trumpeter entitled him to wear the red plume on his spike and he rode a different mount. In fact the only time Henry didn't have Valour as his mount was when he played the trumpet or rode a Drum horse.

Valour couldn't be used as a Drum horse because he was too small to carry the weight of the heavy solid-silver kettle drums. The horses that were used were Clydesdales and they stood 19 hands tall. Although Henry was an experienced rider he had to have further training in the specific use of foot reins. Using his feet and waist to guide the horse enabled him to have his hands free to play the drums. I always felt a lump in my throat when I saw both horse and rider complete. I found myself taking pride in the regiment in a way that I would never have thought possible.

It was 1941 and we were into the second year of the war and approaching the time when decisions had to be made about our future. Army pensions were not sufficient to live on. Henry really had to think about our prospects and an alternative job. As an army family all the house furniture, linen crockery etc. had been provided for us. The price of furnishing our own home came as quite a shock.

We had three months left to sort it all out and we tried to make it a good-natured challenge. We competed to source everything at the best possible price, making a bedroom available in which to store our purchases as we found them. It wasn't easy, as new furniture wasn't being made due to the cut backs of war. Second hand furniture was usually taken by anyone who had lost their homes in the bombing raids. In the scheme of things it wasn't as important for us as it was for those unfortunate souls.

Once again the support from our friends amazed us. They donated all sorts, including their spare curtains and bedding. Henry's mother told us she was sending a couple of boxes to us by Carter Pattison, a haulage company. We were intrigued. If I ventured out, I would ask a neighbour to watch out for them being delivered. A week passed and nothing had arrived. We then received a postcard, informing us that the delivery was scheduled for the following week.

Henry arranged to be there with me. The boxes were extremely heavy and we were grateful that the carriers placed them inside the house. We couldn't wait to unpack them. Layer after layer of paper was wrapped around the contents to protect them. The boxes had been expertly packed. Henry kept repeating, "This is typical of Mama, when she does anything she does it well."

Both of us gasped at the array of china and silver. Mother Taylor had passed all her treasures on to us. Some were her wedding presents and others were gifts from previous employers when she had left their service. I sat on the floor and felt quite choked. Henry joined me. We were overwhelmed by her love and generosity. My initial thought was that everything she had given us was far too precious to use but enclosed within one of the parcels was a note. It read, '*Children please use these, don't put them away as I did.*' It was as though her presence was with us.

We spent the whole evening talking about the life she had had since being widowed. It had been hard for her to remain strong and independent. We both felt nothing but admiration for her wonderful achievement as many others would have failed at such a challenge.

As we talked about Henry's mother, I plucked up courage to mention something that had been bothering me for some time. I asked Henry if he knew why his mother had never divulged to me the fact that he was already married. She was such an honest and sincere woman. Our relationship was now extremely close which made it all the harder to understand. At the time it really hurt that she hadn't told me the truth.

"It was because I begged her not to disclose it until I had found the right time to tell you. As you know only too well, that time didn't arise. Unfortunately, you found out in the most traumatic way. Even now I cannot believe that you forgave me. When I last saw Mama I promised that I would explain the dilemma that I had placed her in. Shamefully, none of this is to my credit. I also failed to carry out her request to tell you. I have no excuse, other than I didn't want to resurrect the past."

Sadly Henry's mother died unexpectedly six months later. By the time she admitted to herself that she was unwell, cancer had spread throughout her body. Henry had visited her the week before she died. I was so pleased that he had been able to tell her that he loved and respected her and that she had always been a beacon in his life.

Mother Taylor's funeral took place ten days later. As you would expect, I accompanied Henry. We were both pleased that she had died relatively quickly and that she didn't have a prolonged and painful death. Morphine eased her passing and she had died in the home that she loved so much.

Sir Richard had asked Henry if he could have the privilege of arranging the funeral service, affirming for Henry that his mother held a special place in the heart of the Walters family. It was planned and executed magnificently. The coffin was carried by the male members of the family and household. Most were in uniform, some on leave and others awaiting their call up. The light oak coffin exited via the very steps that Henry's mother had sat on when waiting to greet him with his letter of acceptance from the military school.

Henry gazed ahead at the tree lined path which

appeared to continue forever, like a never ending ribbon.

"Go with our love Mama."

Sixteen

It was the end of February 1941 and we were both conscious that time was advancing at an alarming pace. Henry's last year at the barracks had sped by and our search for new accommodation wasn't as simple as we thought it would be. All our friends were trying to help us but even so it was proving impossible.

One particular Monday morning Joyce came into work with a beaming smile on her face. Apparently, she'd heard over the weekend that a family friend was going to leave Slough for the remainder of the war. Her husband had been posted abroad and it was her intention to secure her house and move to Newquay to live with her parents. If Henry and I were interested in renting it, Joyce would put in a good word and introduce us. This she did and an agreement was made for us to rent the property with immediate effect.

It was a three bedroom semi detached in Caernarfon Road. We couldn't believe our luck. It would be such a relief for me as I couldn't wait to get out of the barracks and it was away from London. It wasn't a long way out but enough to distance ourselves from the bombing thus reducing our stress. We could both walk to the station and if the train was running, I could catch it to Paddington, a short bus journey from where I worked.

Henry had been assisted in finding a job by the National Association for Employment of Regular Sailors, Soldiers and Airmen. He had a choice of position, either a porter or a postman. He chose the latter. My job was always safe and permanent. It all seemed to be too good to be true. Everything had slotted into place and we knew we would be safely housed for the next couple of years or so.

We packed up our home. All our breakables were wrapped in newspaper and carefully placed in tea chests or boxes. Mother Taylor's treasures were re- packed in the original carrier boxes with the same care. We were longing to display her gifts to us because we wanted them be shown to their best advantage. The move was well thought out by Henry's army friends and was executed with efficiency. Our new abode was only 4 miles from Windsor which enabled us to make several journeys prior to moving day. Moving home this time was not as stressful as it had been on previous occasions.

With every moment accounted for in preparation for the move, we hadn't noticed Henry's discharge day creeping up on us. Henry had mixed emotions about it, as his entire adult life had been dictated by the army. Farewell parties were given in his honour. It was a fitting end to his career and he deserved the accolades he was given.

Henry found that his last few days in the Life Guards passed slowly. Valour, his horse had already been retired three years previously. That separation had been a painful experience for Henry, even though he knew Valour's final years were to be spent in the idyllic surroundings of the army's haven for retired horses, being cosseted for the rest of his life. Had Henry been able, he would have bought his beloved horse. Although Henry had only worked with Clarence, his new horse, for three years, he still found the parting stressful. What amazed me most about Henry was that he revealed more emotions at being parted from his horses than he did from his friends.

Caernarfon Road was a very much sort after area to live in. Semi detached houses lined either side of the road and all of them appeared to be well maintained. We were delighted to reside there. It was everything that we hoped for. My supreme wish was that we could put the more troubled side of our lives to rest. We both needed to look forward and not dwell on the past.

Our good fortune of living away from London was emphasised nightly as we witnessed the bombardment of the East End. We could hear the bombs and see the flames from the back garden as they rose high in the sky above London. It was frightful. The Blitz, as it was so called, was destroying our beautiful city. Our hearts went out to those unfortunate people living and working there. London was bombed the most heavily but there were devastating raids on eighteen other British cities, towns, ports and industrial production centres. I could see the annihilation of London when I travelled to work each morning. That was, if the trains to Paddington, were running. During the course of World War II over one million buildings in London alone were destroyed or damaged by the German Luftwaffe.

Letters from Thomas, my son serving in South Africa, arrived in batches. I often received several in one delivery. It seemed that the war was hardly affecting that part of the world. The tone of Thomas's letters changed from him being homesick and missing us, to him being happy and loving his adopted country. I was soon to find the reason for his change in attitude on opening another letter in the same batch. He was in love and wanted to get married to a South African W.A.A.F. (Women's Auxiliary Air Force). It was a lot to take in all at once. He went on to tell us that rumours were circulating about his division being transferred to Egypt.

Further letters, from the same batch, stated that they would be getting married and the wedding would take place in Cairo on 22nd May 1942. So the rumours had proved to be true. The wedding would take place at All Saints Cathedral and they would be in uniform as would most of the guests. A small reception would take place immediately after the church service at the YMCA club. After reading that particular letter the next one told me they were sending a tier of their wedding cake to us.

A large chunk of important family news was contained

in a single batch of letters. The letters had been written months apart so we had to read them in order to make any sense of them . Thomas always addressed his letters to me but would sign off with, '*Remember me to Adolf.*' This was Thomas's nickname for Henry because he sported a small straight moustache. I thought it looked nothing like Hitler's, or come to that Charlie Chaplin's toothbrush moustache but the name stuck and was used by all members of the family other than me.

We never received the wedding cake. I would have thought that with all the shortages of luxury goods in England at the time, the cake would have been devoured en route. I had been sending parcels to Thomas for some time but he suggested in one letter that I stop as there were no shortages in South Africa. Commodities there were much cheaper also.

In due course photographs arrived of the wedding and their arrival made it all the more real. Lillian, the bride, looked a few years older than Thomas. I could only wish them happiness. Henry and I discussed the marriage and thought that they would probably settle in South Africa. Henry could not relinquish the hatred he felt for that country. I had learnt to keep my own counsel on that subject. It had become a no go area and was not up for discussion.

We got such pleasure from living in the house. It really was our pride and joy. We gradually got to meet the families around us and observed something that struck us as rather unusual. We seemed to be surrounded by neighbours with children the same age, even though some of the neighbours were middle aged or older. We were soon enlightened to the fact that the children were evacuees from the East End of London. Poor little things, they had thought that they were at the other end of England, miles from home. Henry managed to find the odd shop that still had sweets to sell and he would buy a bag and put them out of sight in his pocket. When he saw a little child playing in our road he would take the paper bag out and let them choose a sweet. Before long they got to know the time he came home from work and would wait for him to turn the corner, "Mister, mister," they would shout. I can still hear the sound of their eager voices today.

We were uplifted by helping these little children but then saddened at the news that our landlady's husband had been killed in action. Their little children were now without a father. We felt helpless. There was nothing we could do other than to carry on being good tenants, keeping both the house and garden in good order.

Weeks later we received a letter from our landlady stating we could stay in the house for as long as we wished as she had decided to reside in Cornwall permanently, staying close to her family. However, should she change her mind at a later stage she wanted to be free to do so. We understood that she was nervous to commit herself at this early stage. Being at war influenced all decision making.

Father's was now seventy- three and his health was failing with the problems that accompany old age. I remember my last visit to him vividly, even though Henry and I had visited him frequently. Father and I had walked slowly around the garden at Willow Cottage with him leaning on my arm. He was still so proud of his ability to keep it maintained, not realising that it was far from his standard of perfection. Weeds were growing in both the flower beds and the vegetable plots. I loved him too much to tell him. We both played the same game of pretending everything was as it should be.

Molly found Father one morning slumped in his chair with the morning's newspaper flattened against his chest. It looked like he was having one of his catnaps but he had died, peacefully. We were told he had had a heart attack and wouldn't have known much about it. The family were grateful that he had died as he had lived, quietly and dignified. It was a hard time for me.

Time passed, we struggled through to the end the war and rejoiced with the rest of the nation when in 1945 peace was declared.

I didn't know when I would see Thomas again and Henry's son Samuel had long since moved away from his mother's home. Sarah had told Henry that she didn't like the way he was conducting his life and that he was mixing with the wrong type of friends. We didn't know anymore than that and neither did she.

Seventeen

It was the post war years and with it came uncertainty for the future. Many were without jobs and thousands needed housing. Prime Minister Winston Churchill had warned the nation that when the Second World War was over Britain would be left bankrupt and the returning soldier would have nothing to come back to. He was right. There was a very depressing atmosphere. Rationing was still in force and bread which hadn't been rationed during the war had to be rationed due to the bad wheat harvest of 1946.

We muddled along like everyone else. The thought of our landlady returning was constantly at the back of our minds but our biggest concern was for Thomas and Lillian, his new wife. He still hadn't informed us of their intentions relating to their future. His letters to us sometimes inferred that all was not well between them. He also mentioned that Lillian went on trips without him. Henry and I shared a feeling of unease about their relationship. A letter eventually arrived stating that they were coming home to England initially but would eventually be demobbed in Canada. That news was a bit of a shock. Thomas's limited years in Canada were as a child so he knew nothing of the country. I had experienced the aftermath of the First World War and knew all about the pressures of unemployment combined with the lack of housing. It was no different from our own country. With Thomas's grandparents both dead and no contact with his cousins for years, life would be without support from family or friends. I knew from experience that I would not have survived without the Barratts. Letters passed between us and weeks went by before any definite dates or plans were relayed to us.

Usually couples returning to their homeland travelled together. However, there were so many war brides travelling to Canada that the Department of National Defence had to return dependents in stages due to the sheer volume. Wives were designated to arrive in England and husbands would follow within a month. It all sounded so complicated to us. We invited Lillian to stay with us in Slough until she received her departure orders and she accepted. It gave me pleasure to prepare a room in readiness for her arrival but Henry and I felt the anxiety that many parents feel at meeting their new son or daughter-in-laws for the first time, especially as Lillian would be by herself.

Our next letter from Thomas informed us that Lillian wouldn't be staying with us as her orders stated that she had to travel by Air Force organised transport. We were amazed to learn that her new destination was now Scotland. The Canadian government had a holding house there for brides who were awaiting their turn for embarkation to Canada. Henry and I felt disappointed at the aborted stay. We were by then looking forward to meeting our new daughter-in-law. She promised to contact us as soon as she arrived in Scotland. Days turned into weeks and still we had no word from her. Our lives were also on hold with respect to our own future.

We returned from an outing one afternoon to find a message had been pushed through our letter box requesting our immediate presence at the barracks in Windsor. When we arrived the duty officer asked us to step into his office. Loud voices could be heard and someone was crying. We were shocked to find a distressed Lillian. She had forgotten our address in Slough and had decided to wander around the barracks. She had been picked up by the military police as her visit was contrary to army rules and she had coerced a couple of army wives to cover for her. To civilians that arrangement may have been of no consequence but to army personnel it was a flagrant breach of discipline which didn't endear her to Henry.

We managed to sort things out and Lillian returned with us to Slough and stayed for three days. We found the entire visit a strain and tiresome. She made uncomplimentary comments and criticised everything. She commented that all our gardens in England were like the back yards in South Africa. She told us she found it difficult to manage without a private bathroom as she wasn't used to sharing. In short, nothing came up to South African standards. Henry found these comments hard to handle, and it was all he could do to restrain his temper. He could not forget that his father had been killed and buried in Driefontein. A hate for South Africa had been instilled in him by his mother so it wasn't difficult to understand his feelings. I was consequently relieved when Lillian's visit came to an end. My next letter to Thomas made no reference to the criticisms that Lillian had made. If they already had marital problems we didn't wish to add to them. That was my last letter to South Africa. Letters soon arrived from Lillian telling us she was anxious that she hadn't heard from Thomas but we had nothing to tell her as we too hadn't received mail from him.

Weeks turned into three months. Lillian was not only still waiting to hear from Thomas but was also waiting for news of her own sailing date to Canada.

Our last letter to Thomas was returned. This made us feel very apprehensive as it was returned by Air Force Mail which confirmed it was official. We felt helpless. There was nothing we could do other than wait for news from either Lillian or Thomas.

Letters of enquiry came from Lillian begging us to tell her where Thomas was but we had nothing to tell her. It was so mysterious and very worrying.

The following month Lillian was informed by the authorities that she had one month to decide whether to accept the berth that had been allocated to her on the Aquitania. It was the next ship to leave for Canada that was allocated to war brides. What a dilemma she faced. If the Canadian Air Force didn't know where Thomas was, we couldn't possibly know either. Lillian wrote each week begging for news, she was distraught. As with every letter before we couldn't help in any way.

Life for us was once again at its lowest ebb. We could not accept that the military couldn't trace Thomas. After all, he had to be demobbed and transported by them. Months had gone by without us receiving any information. Lillian decided to go to Canada on the Aquitania as she felt that Thomas would be waiting for her there. We hoped that she would be right as it would bring all our worries to an end.

Our last letter from Scotland was no different from all the others. Lillian was convinced that we knew something and that we were keeping it from her but this couldn't have been further from the truth. We still had no news from any quarter. Henry and I were so worn out by this debacle that we both felt that we were in mourning. Henry's son Samuel had disappeared from choice and mine had vanished from the face of the earth without any trace. If the mighty power of the Canadian Forces could not find him, we surely wouldn't be able to.

Lillian arrived in Canada to the shock of having to acknowledge that Thomas wasn't there to meet her. The dream was shattered. It must have been so frightening to be alone and find that there was no one to care or worry about your plight. She knew that she had to be strong and make a future in Canada or return to South Africa. Both options were open to her.

The Canadian authorities told her that she was now a Canadian citizen by marriage and would be accorded the same rights as any serviceman's wife. If she chose to return to South Africa the Canadian government would fund her return. Poor girl, there was no one to advise her. Both her parents were dead and she had no siblings. There wasn't one reason to return to her native country. In her wisdom, she decided to stay in the hope that Thomas would eventually be found.

In the midst of this trauma, Henry contacted various army welfare groups and government departments asking for help in finding Thomas. One officer came to the house to discuss our concerns. He was of the same opinion as us. No one from the armed forces can disappear without trace. He intended to start from the beginning by researching the records from South Africa and follow the trail to England.

We were pleased that at long last we now had somebody to communicate with directly. Although encouraged by what he had to say we were still fearful that Thomas would be found dead. Each day was a waiting game. Lillian had not written for a couple of weeks so we knew that he hadn't turned up in Canada.

Finally a letter arrived from the army officer stating that he had some news for us and would call the following week. How we managed to appear normal to our friends and neighbours was hard to believe.

Before we knew it the Warrant Officer or W.O. as Henry called him, had arrived and was knocking on the door. He didn't waste any time in informing us that Thomas had arrived in England and due to a fault somewhere along the line Lillian hadn't been informed. He went on to say that from this point onwards any documentation would be recorded and retained by the Canadian government. His intention was to hand over his findings to the Canadian immigration department to further their own search. We were so thankful that Thomas was still alive but at the same time mystified as to the reason for his actions.

Immediately after the visit we wrote to Lillian informing her of the latest news. We suggested to her that she approach the Canadian authorities with a request for them to continue the search for Thomas. She took up our suggestion and a new investigation was initiated. It took several months to carry out and the search concluded that Thomas had been recorded as landing in Canada but from there had vanished into thin air.

The case was then placed in the hands of the famous Mounties. It was two years before The Royal Canadian Mounted Police closed the case and gave up searching for him. We had to concede to defeat.

I could only think that Thomas was suffering from amnesia. Henry was of the opinion that it was to do with Thomas's marriage to Lillian. We had to accept that we would never know. Lillian told us that she would write to us occasionally keeping us informed about her life in Canada. We made the same promise to her and we both kept it.

It was now time for Henry and me to make more decisions about our own future. We knew we couldn't stay in Caernarfon Road forever. We had now been tenants for the over a decade and with each year that passed we had feared it may be our last. We discussed the possibility of attempting to find another house. We were not old but getting older and we needed to find a home that would be our own without the fear of being required to vacate it at short notice. We had had a good landlady and she in turn had had good tenants. Henry had maintained both the inside and outside of the property as though we owned it. We decided that honesty was the best policy and told her of our intentions. She understood completely and intended to put the house on the market when we left.

HENRY
1952 -1953

Eighteen

Esther and I realised more than ever that we were in a position to do whatever was best for us. We could move wherever we wanted to as neither of us had parents or children to consider.

Over the past few months we had seen an advertisement in the national papers. Both of us had read it but hadn't mentioned our interest. The same advertisement appeared again the next day when we were sitting down reading the newspapers together. The headline read:

OFFERS
AWAITING INTERESTED PARTIES

A government department called the Development Corporation was offering houses in various counties to people in need of housing.

Esther showed interest in the advertisement and said, "Do you think it's worth us applying?"

"Let's go for it. We've nothing to lose."

In 1946 the New Towns Act was passed by parliament.

It gave the government power to designate areas of land for building new homes. Stevenage, in Hertfordshire, was the first new town with a further ten following by 1955. The new towns were intended to alleviate the housing shortage in London brought about by the Blitz.

It was just what we needed and should we be accepted we would have no problem as to where to live. We liked the sound of a town in Hertfordshire called Hemel Hempstead. As an ex-serviceman I would be eligible. We were both enthusiastic but at the same time fearful that as we lived in Slough it would preclude us from applying. It didn't.

My army status gave us the points we needed. On our application we were given the option of applying for Stevenage or waiting for the finish of Crawley in West Sussex but we had already decided that Hemel Hempstead was the town for us. We had looked it up in an atlas and found that it was surrounded by the Chilterns and had the Grand Union canal flowing through it. It also wasn't far from Slough. We had bought a Morris motorcar with Esther's father's legacy and its purchase had transformed our lives.

We made a plan to visit Hemel Hempstead when we received the tenancy offer. Thousands were on the waiting list but we heard from the Development Corporation within a few months.

The following Sunday after church we sped off with our flask and sandwiches to what we hoped would be our new place of residence. We loved the town because it was a combination of both town and country.

Coaches were parked along the riverbank near the town centre. They were full of prospective applicants surveying their future town and I was sure they were making the same plans as Esther and I. New factories were being opened by large companies and working for one of them made you eligible for housing. I remember thinking, good luck to them.

Large maps had been made available so that prospective new towners could see both the housing and the factory areas which were on the outskirts of the town.

I felt we had been smart because we had looked carefully at the map and searched for a location with the prospect of being able to walk to the town and the attractive parkland. It made us choose an area called Gadebridge. It was named after the River Gade where we had seen the coaches parked alongside the river bank earlier that day.

We drove to find a road with the best position. We hadn't been that clever as so many of the roads and houses were unfinished. We had to do quite a lot of walking but with the help of a few builders who were working on site we found the spot to aim for.

We were fortunate that the builders were working on a Sunday. We chatted to them and they went into the office and told us that the road we were looking at would be called Hillcrest. All the way home Esther was worried that we wouldn't be allocated a house in this road. She had convinced herself that all the houses had been allocated already. We now had to sit tight and wait for the confirmation of our choice.

On several occasions one afternoon I pestered my boss at the sorting office to allow me to use the telephone. I think it was with sheer exasperation at my doggedness that the letting officer of the Development Corporation finally offered us a tenancy. I feigned being ill in an attempt to be sent home. It worked and when I told Esther she was ecstatic. She deserved good news after all the stress she'd had.

We were now into the final three months of my career with the post office and there were a lot of things to organise before the move. At fifty three I was too young to retire and I needed to find another job as I didn't want to travel to Slough each day. I managed to secure a job in the civil service at Hemel Hempstead. It was with the Stationery Office. I couldn’t believe my good fortune as so many people had also applied for the position. It would appear that once again my army career gave me the edge over the other applicants. My length of service followed by a good reference from the G.P.O. sealed the position for me.

Esther intended to retire from her job. She felt the daily commute from Hemel Hempstead to London would be too stressful. She remembered the company's loyalty to her over the years so it was a big decision for her to make.

Our pensions with my moderate salary would enable us to live comfortably. Both of us were astounded by the good wishes we received from all our colleagues. Parties were given in our honour with gifts galore for our new home.

Every free day we had we were in Hemel Hempstead measuring for carpets and curtains, towel rails and such like. Everything Esther said we needed was bought. It felt as though this was our first proper home. I had always lived in homes decorated and furnished by other people – as a child, in service, then with the army for twenty two years and latterly as a tenant in Slough. Our new house in Gadebridge really would be our first private home together.

ESTHER

1953 - 1956

Nineteen

After a restless night we awoke to the realisation that moving day had arrived. Henry and I were pleased to be leaving Caernarfon Road. We jumped out of bed quite quickly, our tiredness was soon forgotten.

A large blue van was parked outside. Henry's friend Tom had managed to borrow it from his company. As I looked down on its roof, from the bedroom window, the notion of us moving away was still hard to believe.

All three of us worked unstintingly and by midday we were exhausted but every single one of our boxes and tea chests was loaded onto the van. As I watched Henry drop the keys through the letter box, the move became a reality.

Tom patted my shoulder. "There's no turning back now girl. Hertfordshire here we come."

Our journey from Slough did not take long. Tom decided to show us the scenic route. We drove through Burnham Beeches which was so beautiful with its trees in the first stages of autumnal colour. Amersham was followed by the small town of Chesham, where we spotted the first road sign, that we were aware of, to Hemel Hempstead. We both shrieked out the name at the same time. We were like unruly children on a school outing. Once we reached Hemel Hempstead we recognised where we were and directed Tom to Gadebridge.

Henry and Tom went to the site office to collect our keys. Henry and I stood at the front door offering each other the keys to open the door officially for the first time. Within the hour another van arrived with all our new pieces of furniture. We were so relieved that we had already arranged for the carpets to be laid and the curtains to be hung. We worked solidly all day and were incredibly grateful to Tom for his untiring help.

As the light faded I unpacked a picnic onto an upturned tea chest and found the kettle, tea and flask of milk which I'd set aside. We were all ravenous and ate the whole lot heartily before bidding Tom farewell.

Sleep came quickly that night. We were grateful to be in our new house with the majority of our possessions unpacked.

It was such an unreal feeling when we awoke the next morning. We had to get our bearings. We had woken up in the same bedroom for the past ten years. I made my way over to the window and drew the curtains to confirm that all was as it should be. Yes, the green of the park was visible to my right and the hubbub from the building site was coming from my left, all was as before. Our new home felt like perfection to us both.

Henry had two weeks free before he started his new job. That first morning we ate our cereal and toast leisurely while making a list of all the various jobs which needed to be done. We then prioritised them.

Paths were needed to both the back and front of the property. Henry took himself off to appraise the availability of any surplus paving. His perseverance paid off. Broken paving stones were being sold at 3d per builder’s barrow load. He was as delighted with his purchase as if he had won the football pools.

While I sat writing change of address letters, Henry laid the stone slabs. I kept seeing the top of his head pass by the window. I was mystified as to where he was going and the reason why? I got up to find out what he was up to and blocked his path. His protests of, "Quick, out of my way. Don’t stop me," were justified. He was wheeling a barrow load of wet cement. Once again the builders had turned up trumps.

Within a week crazy paving pathways enhanced both the front and back gardens or what would eventually be a front and back garden. At that stage it looked more like builder's rubble with a scant layer of top soil.

We gradually ticked off things on our 'To Do' list and achieved our goals one by one. During Henry’s second week off he hung pictures on the walls, put up shelving for books, put shelving in the airing cupboard and did all the little jobs that wives find for their husbands to do.

I was thankful to wave Henry off to work the following Monday. I wished him good luck and sent him on his way with a big kiss and hug. To my shame I felt a sense of relief. I wanted time by myself not only to assess our new home but to reflect on how I would use my newly found free time. I had worked for so many years with the clock governing my life. For decades I had filled my days with other people's needs. Now time was mine to fill as I wished.

I decided to venture out to celebrate my first day of freedom. I wanted to explore the area and autumn was in its full splendour.

Noise from the builders creating more houses diminished as I walked away. I hadn't strolled far down the hill before I noticed green rolling fields across the valley. I assumed these hills were part of the Chilterns. Anyhow, they made a splendid back drop to the trees in the park which were shedding their leaves and towering above a carpet of colour. It was rather lovely and was only yards from my home. All I had to do was to walk down the hill and cross a little road.

Approaching the park I became aware of a flash of white glinting under the trees. As I got nearer, I could see it was an old wrought iron bridge crossing the river, which Henry had told me was the River Gade. As I sauntered over the bridge I ran my hands over the iron rail and thought of all the people that had probably done the same over the years. Quite unexpectedly my emotions got the better of me and I wanted to run back to the house. Everything was overwhelming and I found it difficult to handle. So much of my adult life had been negative and I found life's pleasures harder to cope with. I didn't return home but pulled myself together and ambled on through the park alongside the river bank.

There were so many shoals of minnows and stickle-backs darting in and out of the plants in the river. The water was so clear that I would have been happy to drink it. As I watched its fast flow, I wondered where it came from and where it flowed to.

I kept turning around not knowing where to look next. I walked on through the fallen leaves, crunching them under foot. The noise seemed amplified, something quite extraordinary and not a sound I had previously heard. It made me really aware of what I was doing and I felt I needed to apologise to the leaves for disturbing them. I passed several other people walking their dogs, a number of which were playing around the base of the trees making lots of yapping noises. I turned to watch them and as I did, slipped over and fell in a heap. My fall was cushioned by the mounds of leaves. In seconds help was at hand and I was back on my feet with no harm done.

Much good came from my little accident. A group who obviously knew each other, formed around me. There must have been six or seven of them, two retired gentlemen and the rest middle aged women. Conver-sation flowed as they enquired after me and asked if I would like someone to see me home. I told them I had only lived in the town for two weeks. They made me feel welcome to their town and with farewells of, "Hope to see you again," I made my way further into the park.

I discovered a walled garden on the far side of the park. Benches were secreted around the formal flower-beds. Each had a plaque, most in memoriam, telling of the deceased person's interest in the garden and how they had enjoyed its sanctuary. I sat on one of the seats and closed my eyes.

Rested, I left the garden through a stone porch way. I couldn't make up my mind if it was a genuine ruin or a folly. I lagged behind some dog walkers who had left shortly before me and I followed them out of the park through a different exit. I made the decision to turn left and keep parallel with the park in order not to get lost. The road twisted gently uphill and became narrower. Next to the park's exit was a large shop with the sign Bellman's. It had been converted into a small factory. I could hear a mechanical whirring coming from within and it was accompanied by the sound of girls singing. It was a small clothing company, next to which was a photographer's shop with an adjoining bank.

I looked up the hill. Many of the shops seemed to have their original features and there were more old buildings in the distance. Across the road was a Woolworth's store. The shop's frontage had striking bow windows which appeared to be in a mahogany frame with F. W. WOOLWORTH in large gold letters. High on the wall next to the shop was a street sign - *High St.*

"So this is the heart of Hemel Hempstead," I said out loud. And I had found it by myself.

As I climbed the hill I passed a couple of pubs which

looked as if they had been frozen in time. Within a couple of minutes a splendid building with impressive arches stood to my left. Through the arches I could partially see St Mary's church, which had dominated the park with its tall elegant lead spire. Adjacent was the market square where markets were held every Thursday and Saturday. To the right of the square, on the corner, was the public library. How delightful to think that you could choose a book and leave by a dozen steps into the park and read to the sound of the birds' song.

I had to sit once more to rest. My brain was spiralling from all the things I had seen. How interesting my first day had been. I couldn't wait for Henry to return home. I realised that I must let him tell me about his first day at work before I told him of my day's happenings. However old or experienced you are, starting a new job can be formidable.

I was delighted when I saw Henry returning from work and walking towards the house. He too was pleased and couldn't wait to sit down and tell me about his day.

Apparently, on his arrival at the office he had been introduced to his new colleagues and this had taken a considerable chunk out of the morning. It was all very informal, they had then chatted to him, relating their various stories about how they had come to settle in Hemel Hempstead. Like ourselves a lot of Henry's colleagues had moved to gain new employment and with it a chance to obtain a new house and a better future for their families. Henry thought that in a strange way it was rather like the camaraderie of the barracks. It was such a good beginning. Walking home through Gadebridge Park had rounded off his first day nicely. We hugged each other tightly and sat there soaking in the moment before I shared my wonderful day with him.

We were now both sleeping well and our lives were in tune in every way. After breakfast the following morning Henry made his way through the park to his place of work and I accompanied him part of the way. I had decided to do something to surprise him that evening. It was my intention to visit the library so I could find out as much as possible about the town.

I was too early. The library hadn't opened its doors so I used the spare time, whilst I waited, to look at the rest of the High Street. The pavement dropped low to the left with attractive black iron railings above. Tall Georgian houses backed onto the park and a few had small shops on their ground floors. I climbed a flight of steps to regain access to road level where I crossed and walked back down the other side. I found it as charming as before. Although I had been used to Windsor and its old historic buildings, the High Street was much smaller and seemed more cosy and quaint. It was definitely an improvement on Slough.

As I had hoped, when I retraced my steps to the library, it was open. I left much later with several books on the history of the town plus much information gleaned from the librarian. Why Hemel Hempstead was referred to as a new town was surprising. My books informed me that it was a market town and was granted a Royal Market Charter from Henry VIII in 1539.

Later that night I shared with Henry all I had learned. He was as interested as me to discover that Henry VIII's love affair with Ann Boleyn might have been conducted in the town. Supposedly, the renowned Walled Garden with its Charter Tower derives its name from another local myth. It was thought that Henry VIII might have stayed there in 1539 and handed down Hemel Hempstead's charter from the upper window, as a mark of gratitude for the hospitality he had received. This would have to have been from a previous tower, as the existing one wasn't built until after that date but we both thought it an intriguing story.

At the end of each day I was inspired to plan my next. We both shared this interest and Henry said he had never felt so contented in his life.

As on previous mornings I walked with Henry, for part of his journey to work, through the park and we shared the splendour of it all with one another. We said our farewell. I kissed him on the cheek and as we parted I quickened my step with the anticipation of what I was about to do. I had noticed a specialist shop the day before and since then I had been in a quandary as to what I should do. I decided to act on my impulse and I bought a bicycle.

I chose a very basic one, as I had no knowledge of gears. My choice was a Raleigh. The owner of the cycle shop assured me that they were well built and very suitable for ladies. I was then duly measured for the height of my saddle and handlebars. I paid and was soon on my way home with my new purchase.

I rode through the park grinning, like the cat that had got the cream. This indulgence would enable me to venture further afield to pastures new. I couldn't wait for my adventures to start. I would get a map of the local area and list all the places that I could ride to and return within a day.

Henry remarked on his arrival home that my face was like a child's at Christmas. As if to prove that our relationship had developed into something special he added, "I knew you were up to something when we walked through the park this morning. You walked with a spring in your step."

It is observations like these that are the true foundations of a marriage. It's not always a gift of roses that counts. All the concerns that I had previously worried about regarding our families were now slowly receding.

Henry confessed to me that amongst the many boxes yet to be unpacked, that were stored in either the garage or the shed, were numerous motor cycle parts. I was amazed as I had never heard him once mention the fact. He certainly hadn't conveyed to me his interest in motor bike racing. I was pleased for him to have this extra interest. He declared his intention to restore the bike to its original condition. We laughed together at the thought of us careering around the country lanes.

Our future was now meandering like a river, flowing

purposefully but with its twists and turns beyond our sight.

Weeks then months were spent with Henry laying pieces of metal over every available outside space. Paths were impassable to access the clothes line. Winter was imminent and Henry was concerned that all the parts had to be connected before the heavy rains or snows fell. I couldn't envisage this ever happening.

Once again I was proved wrong. Henry, with the help of a few of his office colleagues worked every available spare moment. It was nearing completion but it didn't look like the shape of a regular motor bike, well not to me. Henry defended the bike as though it was his baby. I kept getting told that it would be worth a fortune when it was finished. Apparently, it was a vintage bike, a 1930 BSA 250cc B30-4. I still wasn't impressed. The motor-bike became Henry's love and obsession. He had little time for his music and also spent less time with me.

December arrived and with it the complete restoration of the bike. It stood there in all its glory. The chrome shining brightly, lovingly polished by Henry, who had to be the most experienced and accomplished polisher of all. As we all stood around the BSA giving it admiring looks Henry came out with a tray of glasses, accompanied by a bottle of Champagne. It was for the whole team to share before the big rev up. Bizarrely, it was quite emotional. When the glasses were raised Henry turned the key. The noise was deafening. It sounded as though a stadium of bikes were revving up. She was off and Henry, proud as a mother who had just given birth, rode off with the cheers of the team and all our new neighbours. Champagne was offered to everybody. It was wonderful and such an achievement.

My two wheels were a different story. I had no fear of engine failure or a lack of petrol. Owning our own set of wheels gave us our personal freedom. With respect to Henry's machine, he wanted to run it in before he allowed pillion passengers. I cycled locally for a month or two, finding new estates. All my discoveries lead me to believe that we had chosen our location wisely.

Daily we related our day's comings and goings to each other. We had both been used to fairly structured lives and this new freedom required some adjustment by us both. Although Henry worked hard it was very different from what he was used to. He said his office was relaxed and he even had time to discuss the politics of the day.

On week days I continued my habit of walking half way through the park with Henry. We always greeted the same people walking their dogs. It was on one of these occasions that the seed of an idea was planted. We both loved dogs so why didn't we get one of our own? That very evening we searched The Gazette, the local paper, for information. Sure enough, a dog rescue centre wasn't too far from us. It was near to a familiar route, the one we had taken when we used to visit Gadebridge from Slough. We contacted the rescue centre and arranged a visit.

There were so many dogs to choose from. I felt sorry for them all and could easily have walked away with most of them. It really was a heart searching decision to make. Tessa won us over with her persuasive dark brown eyes. She captured our hearts. She was a three year old Labrador cross with a light brown coat.

An anxious week followed before we were allowed to collect her. On our arrival back at the kennel she appeared to remember us and we were greeted with squeals, barks and licks. We made a connection immediately and became the best of friends. Tessa brought such happiness to us.

Henry's walks to work took on a new significance. We had to allow more time for greetings from other dog owners and the curiosity of their dogs. Our circle of friends once again extended. Before too long we were on first names terms with our fellow dog walking companions. Lovely Tessa gave us so much pleasure. When my health deteriorated she remained placid, sitting quietly by my side. It was as if she sensed life was changing and she adapted, curtailing her exuberance. Henry said that when he walked her, as soon as they reached the park she reverted back to a lively dog full of energy.

It was a very ordinary morning. I was a lot later leaving the house than usual for my daily cycle ride. The postman greeted me at the front door and handed over a large white envelope. On the front was an outsized label showing several addresses. The letter appeared to have been redirected several times and a '*return to sender if unknown at this address*' was also attached. I managed to decipher our last two addresses, written underneath. The address before last was handwriting I recognised. It was Thomas's and the frank mark was Canada.

I shook so badly, my heart raced, my trembling knees gave way and I slid onto the floor in the hallway. It took me a while before I could get up and compose myself enough to tackle opening the envelope. I was so afraid that I would damage not only the envelope but the enclosed letter as I was still shaking and in such an unstable condition. Over the years I had fantasised about such an occurrence but when it came I wasn't prepared. I sat in an arm chair in the sitting room and gingerly pulled the letter out. Thomas's words were implausible for the period of time that he had been missing, presumed dead. It was as if he was writing after a few months not years. He began by saying, '*It has been a long time since you heard from me*.' He continued, '*I am now discharged and have a job with a frozen food company working as a salesman.'*

He was living in a place called Cornwall and was sure that I would remember it, as it was on the St Laurence River. Thomas went on to inform us that he had not heard from Lillian for a long time. His letter harked back to his job stating that he was a travelling salesman for this company and if he could get shareholders, called unit holders in Canada, to buy more shares he would end up a wealthy man. It was so confusing. He then requested that we didn't inform Lillian that he had contacted us.

It was such a mess. I felt ashamed that my son could

write in such a way, with no apologies or reasons for his disappearance. My life shattered and I felt traumatised once again. How could I have produced a child without any shred of shame or concern for the people who loved him?

Our letter to Lillian the previous month had been sent with all honesty. Now I was left with the decision of whether to tell her that I had heard from Thomas.

I was physically sick and had no control over my shaking. I had such a short time to compose myself before Henry returned home from work. I decided I couldn't tell him immediately. I felt mortified and humiliated by my son's atrocious behaviour. Perhaps it would be for the best if I wrote to him first to glean more information.

It was then that I realised, I too, like Lillian, had no forwarding address.

Twenty

Henry was his usual cheery self when he returned home from work. He would have expected me to greet him with my usual kiss and hug but I couldn't rise from the chair. He looked concerned and immediately enquired, "Do you feel ill? You look dreadful. Have you fallen off your bicycle?"

It was all said in a rush of anxiety.

I looked up at him and managed to gasp out, "I haven't been out as I feel so ill."

Naturally, Henry wanted to send for the doctor. In my effort to prevent that from happening I became hysterical. Poor Henry didn't know what to do. He made one last brave attempt to calm me down and placate me.

"Just breathe deeply, slowly does it. Try not to worry. Perhaps it's … err, it might be what some women call the change of life."

There I had my solution. I agreed telling him that I too had heard that some women my age go through the same experience. I was in the right age bracket at fifty-four but I was lying.

I went to bed but sleep evaded me. My brain was working overtime. Henry had offered to move into the spare bedroom in an effort to give me more space. I was extremely grateful as it meant I could talk to myself, cry and pace around the floor of the bedroom without having to account for my actions. Eventually I drifted in and out of sleep.

The night was long but morning inevitably came. I re-read Thomas's letter again. It took some time for me to get my head around this appalling story. I felt that once again my son's actions had brought me great distress. It was like an unseen torture.

Days passed into weeks and months with still no further news from Canada. Henry had observed my depression and steady decline but was completely unaware of the dilemma I faced. I still couldn't bring myself to tell him that I had heard from Thomas. I felt too ashamed of my son.

My weight plummeted by the day. Henry persistently begged and pleaded with me to see a doctor but I stubbornly dug my heels in and resisted. I knew deep down that I needed professional help. I was apprehensive that seeking medical advice would result in me having to confide my inner turmoil to someone and this would in turn lead to me having to tell Henry.

The decision was taken out of my hands. I collapsed in the house and was admitted to hospital. I had suffered a cardiac arrest. A week passed before I became aware that I was in hospital. The skills of the doctors and intensive care team had saved my life. It was a couple of days afterwards that the horror of the story wormed its way back into my brain. Nothing had been resolved or gone away.

One month on I was discharged into the care of my husband. Both physiotherapists and occupational therapists visited me at home to assess my needs. Forms were then completed and sent to the appropriate places in order to make my life easier. One thing I wasn't able to master was the stairs, which meant my bedroom was now in the sitting room. My thoughts were constantly in a commotion and I realised I needed some sort of psychological therapy but I couldn't bring myself to ask for help. I couldn't divulge my innermost secret or unlock it to reveal any part of it to anybody.

Henry was still blissfully ignorant to the fact that I had received a letter from Thomas. Months went by and I was prepared to accept that I would never hear from Thomas again.

A home help was sent to assist me with the chores I was no longer able to do. She was a thin angular woman called May. On this particular morning she brought me, as usual, my coffee and digestive biscuit on a tray but lying next to the mug was an air letter. I immediately recognised the Canadian stamp.

I was fearful that my racing heart would escalate into a cardiac arrest again. I breathed deeply and slowly and calmed myself down. May was consumed with curiosity and her requests for me to open the letter went unheeded.

As soon as she left, I took a sip of brandy from the glass on the mantelpiece and I opened the aerogram with trembling hands.

As with the previous letter I'd received, Thomas began by saying, *"I am sorry I have not written for a while."*

My son went on to inform me that he now had another job and was once again finding himself short of money. It was his intention to write to Lillian suggesting a divorce. The divorce would be based on the fact that Lillian had not been fulfilling her wifely duties. His words not mine. It was unbelievable. As far as I knew he did not have Lillian's address and hadn't a clue as to where she lived.

At least I now had an address where I could write to him. Thomas sounded like a person suffering from delusions. I couldn't begin to imagine how I was going to answer or advise him in my reply. This latest letter was as disjointed as the preceding one. I felt nauseous and my head started to spin.

What a quandary I was in. I still hadn't revealed any of this to Henry and it was beginning to make me feel guilty again. Once more I went downhill swiftly and my recovery was impeded by my son yet again.

My doctor was baffled by this set back and sought a second opinion from a consultant. This was enough to make me feel guilty and ashamed of my behaviour. During the consultation at the hospital I broke down, cried and confessed to the doctor what had happened to my son and also that I had not told my husband about the letter I had received. He was so considerate and understanding, and referred me to a counsellor. During the first counselling session the doctor suggested that the trauma I had been through was no different from bereavement.

I now felt ready to confess all to Henry. He was understandably hurt at being excluded from Thomas's reappearance in our lives. He understood my shame however. It was a relief to share my burdens with him at last. Now that I no longer had to shoulder the worries and concerns by myself I started to recover. Although a slow process, I was on the up, health wise.

Again months went by without an answer to my letter. We had almost given up on hearing from Thomas but in the fullness of time a letter did arrive. He made no reference to hearing from me or that he had contacted Lillian, only the fact of being in love. He had met a wonderful woman who loved him and wanted to spend the rest of her life with him. He was everything that she was looking for. This had to support my theory that Thomas was unbalanced. There was no history or stability in his letters. Thomas seemed to flit from one thing to another. What was mentioned in one letter was never referred to again in another. I replied by return stating my disapproval.

A decision had to be made as to whether or not we would inform Lillian. It was only fair to do so. We hadn't acted on this when a letter arrived from Lillian. It was surreal. In it she had enclosed a legal document which stated that she could apply for Thomas to be presumed legally dead as it was now 1953 and seven years had elapsed since his disappearance. She went on to inform us that she had been notified by the Royal Canadian Mounted Police that they could find no trace of him. It was now official.

What timing. It placed us in such a predicament. Two days after hearing from Lillian my letter to Thomas was returned stating '*Not known at this address*'. We were back to square one and were now being drawn into this web of deceit. Surely all these lies and dramas were not contrived solely for the purpose of leaving his wife? A simple, 'I'm leaving for good,' would have been all that was needed.

Eventually more letters arrived from Thomas each from a different address. In one he confessed to being sued in a paternity case, in others he begged for money. Henry had no idea that I had already sent him money by international transfer on several occasions. Thomas had known exactly how to manipulate me. All his letters were full of contradictions and lies. One lie gave birth to the dozens that followed. Pathological liars believe the stories they tell. My son was very sick.

His story of the paternity case was a cover story. That particular lie would have been said in the hope that Lillian would divorce him. Letters he claimed to have written to Lillian would have been sent to a fictitious address. His girl friend would have believed it all. I cannot find the words to describe his behaviour. Both

Henry and I supposed that his new girl friend would have believed that Thomas was doing all he could to straighten out his life. Such was his skill. He was a cunning and devious liar.

We continued to write to Lillian. We were amazed at how she had turned her life around. My son was a user of people and always needed to confirm his lies. If only he had used his devious brain for good he would have been successful and could have created a good life for himself and his family.

I was never to hear from my son again. We did relate all the news to Lillian. She endeavoured for some time to find him, even employed a private detective but it was to no avail. Nothing was heard from him again by anybody.

LILLIAN

1945 - 1983

Twenty-one

Letters came regularly from Esther and 'Adolf,' as I still called Thomas. I felt despondent when I read them most of them. It must have been so difficult for Esther to acknowledge that her son was a real swine. I had to give up my search for Tommy. Eventually Esther signed a 'presumed dead' document for me. The Canadian authorities had done all in their power to trace him.

Happily, my life became different after I became a Christian. I left all my troubles with God and it worked for me, for most of the time. I was in control of my life once again. I had many friends in my community, some of whom were work colleagues. Whilst I was waiting in Scotland for repatriation I worked for an insurance company and that experience stood me in good stead for selection in Canada. My occupation enabled me to support myself financially.

During my childhood I had developed a great love of the piano. I was just six years old when I started to learn to play. When I received a salary again, as a civilian in Ontario, my first luxury present to myself was a new piano. I had heard of a marvellous pianist who would only take pupils he felt were talented. You were tested then accepted or rejected on the spot. You had to play a very difficult piece that he had composed himself. I was so fortunate to be taught by this talented man for many years until I had gained every certificate possible. I was now able to teach the piano and select my own pupils.

I was offered promotion at work which meant it was time for me to make a momentous decision about my life. I had to either give up my job or refrain from teaching. In the end there was no contest. Music was now my whole life.

I endeavoured to keep my previous life and its tribulations a thing of the past although this was very difficult. I felt I could never forgive Tommy for what he had put me through. We had had our ups and downs in our short marriage but I couldn't work out why someone would chose to go missing.

I now frequented concerts and played in others, socialising with like minded people who shared in my passion. One special friend, Dorothy, would often come over to my apartment and have supper with me. Our friendship grew. We had a lot in common and spent more and more time together including touring holidays. We both liked to travel and enjoyed every moment of our together time on the road. On one of these trips we decided to share a home together. In some ways it seemed such a big step but we were both middle aged and knew full well what we were doing.

We had a fantastic time viewing property. Our joint incomes enabled us to purchase a house and bid farewell to our small apartments. We found a delightful house on the outskirts of Bancroft. I kept thanking God for this miraculous change and good fortune in my life. Dorothy was not religious but conceded that someone appeared to be looking after us.

At last my life had become fulfilled. We supported each other and had a reason to get up each morning and be grateful for whatever the day would bring. We had no hassle from families about our living arrangements as Dorothy, like me, was an only child and her parents had also passed on years before. We both worked diligently at our respective jobs and our relaxation came from walking and tending our attractive garden. I still taught music most days but played the piano every evening for my own enjoyment, moreover I knew Dorothy got pleasure from listening to every note.

Later on in our retirement, arthritis took its toll on Dorothy. Household chores, long walks and gardening became a thing of the past. Thank goodness we were still able to go for short drives. Ontario in the fall was beyond description. It didn't take us long to drive to Algonquin Park. The red oaks, aspens, and tamaracks reached their peak in October. We both appreciated gazing at the majesty of the trees with the carpets of colour adorning their bases. We often travelled in silence sharing the peace and tranquillity.

This way of life helped me to deal with the many

ghastly memories that continually smouldered within me. Rejection is nigh on impossible to come to terms with. It is an inner battle that many people have to accept. Hard that it is, you ultimately have to let it go, otherwise it prevents you from accepting life everyday with all the gifts that it can bring. Thankfully my religion enabled me to let go and share my love with my new partner. As I grew older I often reflected on my childhood in the Cape but I had no wish or reason to revisit South Africa. I had no family left in the country. I would be a tourist in a city that I once knew so well. I felt strongly that a visit would be detrimental and result in happy childhood memories being eradicated forever.

In February 1979 I received a letter from England in an unknown handwriting. I was curious and impatient to open it. It was from a woman called Jane, informing me that both of my in-laws had died. It came as a shock but it was a warm letter explaining how death had quietly crept up on them both within a short space of time. Although we hadn't always had the closest of relationships I was thankful to read that both their deaths were peaceful.

I wrote back to Jane within the week and over time we exchanged quite a few letters. I learned that she had worked for the district nursing service and it was through her nursing Esther that she got to know both Esther and Adolf. Jane had explained that long after she had resigned from her job she had kept a watchful eye on them. I was astounded to read that during this time Jane and her family had moved to Durban for just over a year. I am sure that my in-laws found that very hard to accept knowing their hatred of the country. I know a barrier existed between us, especially with my father-in-law, when he found out I was South African. At least I had been prepared for their hostile attitude by Tommy, who had filled me in on Henry's father's death at Driefontein.

Another door on the past had been closed. The following years were unkind to Dorothy. She had become much frailer and had the added burden of diabetes. My heart ached watching her suffering but she carried it with fortitude until her death.

When Dorothy finally died I was inconsolable. This astounding woman had shared her love and life with me. We had no secrets between us and had shared everything. I missed her so much. I questioned my faith, lost my spirit and found for almost a year I couldn't play the piano.

On one sunny afternoon the following spring whilst I was sitting in my armchair having one of my usual catnaps, I heard Dorothy talking to me. She whispered, "Get up now and go and play your piano."

I was convinced that she had actually spoken to me. I sat on my piano stool and played the first piece of music that I stumbled upon. As I played, tears flooded down my cheeks and onto the keys of the piano. The music had released my pain. After that occasion every time I missed Dorothy I would play the piano, just for her.

I knew I would have to write to Jane and tell her of Dorothy's death, she would want to know.

ESTHER

1957 - 1974

Twenty-two

Our lives were ticking along nicely since our move to Hemel Hempstead. This new way of living was so different. I appreciated the time I had to myself and would often reflect on my childhood, appreciating the bounty that had surrounded me, my parents' protective love and security. These thoughts took me in turn to remembering my sister Molly.

How had it happened that we were no longer in contact? We had been so supportive of each other during our childhood and the early days of our marriages. I had to think hard to recall what had started the rift between us. How could I have allowed all this time from father's death until now to put a wrong right. It was such a stupid thing to fall out over. When Father had died thirteen years ago he had left more of his personal belongings to me than he had to Molly. She was hurt for sure and I should have understood and not been so insensitive.

I was fifty-eight and thought I should make amends before even more time passed between us. I wrote a letter saying it was such stupid thing that had come between us and that I still loved her and asked her to forgive me. I also told her I felt ashamed of myself for allowing such a situation to exist, especially as she and Jim had been my biggest support upon my return from Canada and at the time of Roger's passing.

An answer came by return post. Molly said that she and Jim, her husband, had been over the moon at receiving news from us. She wrote, "*I cannot see the paper for my tears of joy.*" Her blotted dried tears were evident on the writing paper. Henry was as delighted as I was that Molly had replied so quickly. We sorted out a weekend that we had free the following month but then decided we couldn't wait that long and juggled our diary around so that we could visit them the next Sunday. As we had transport it had been left to us to decide when we would travel down to Kent. Breaking the ice by letter had made me impatient to see them.

The picturesque villages and countryside of Kent looked charming in the sunshine. My thoughts went straight back to Willow Cottage. I nearly asked Henry to make a slight detour via West Farleigh so we could drive past the cottage but decided against it. I wanted my memories of the place to remain untouched. Molly and Jim were now living in a bungalow in Yalding. We arrived in time for lunch. Molly opened the door to greet us and we instantly flung our arms around each other without breathing a word. Our hugs then blended with the tears that flowed. Nonstop chatting and catching up took us through the day. Molly had problems breathing as she was suffering from Emphysema. I was concerned that my sister was struggling. Any activity seemed to cause her problems.

Molly, like any concerned auntie wanted to know the latest news of Thomas. I didn't want to add to her burden but she whispered, "Please don't exclude me," then gulped for more air, "I want to know everything about him and his wife."

I related everything to her, leaving nothing out. Both Molly and Jim found it all hard to believe and interjected with comments such as, "This isn't the Thomas we knew. How could he have done such a dreadful thing to you?" Finally Molly said, "Oh Esther, poor you. Thank you for telling us. Now I don't feel excluded from family matters." She paused to catch her breath, "I want to be involved and help."

I realised just how precious my sister was to me and that this estrangement must never happen again. Before we left we arranged for them to visit us. Molly and Jim hadn't visited Hemel Hempstead before so it would all be new to them. Henry volunteered to collect them.

Two weeks later he set off very early and drove to Kent to be there for 9 o'clock, straight after their breakfast. It would give them a longer day with us. As I prepared the lunch Henry drove Molly and Jim a short distance to Ashridge, a local beauty spot. They were fortunate to see a herd of deer grazing outside Ashridge House, a 19th century neo-gothic mansion with centuries of history. They were captivated and Henry made a promise to them that we would all return in warmer weather for a picnic.

Our closeness was magnified into a strength I couldn't explain only feel. Talking to Molly about Thomas had helped me. Unlike Henry she had the empathy of a mother. In fairness to Henry he was much more pragmatic and realistic about the whole situation. He saw it for what it was, a son deceiving his mother.

The whole experience with Molly made me appraise myself. I felt guilty and sorry for the hurt my attitude had caused to various people. I promised myself that I would try to be a nicer person in the future.

Henry and I both became keen gardeners. In my case it was a resurrection of a previous love. Gardening was good for my health. I was out in the fresh air. My doctor had informed me that gentle exercise would benefit my heart. Father's handed down skills had been lying dormant inside me and I rediscovered how addictive gardening could be. As a gardener you treasure the seasons as they arrive as each one brings its own beauty, even the stark cold of winter. Every year the local authority gave prizes to the best tended gardens. We tried on many occasions but the prize always alluded us. To make us feel better I would quote the old maxim, 'it's not the winning, it's the taking part that counts.' Nevertheless, it didn't console us.

As the neighbourhood grew and developed, purpose built community centres organised clubs and activities. One was in our locality at Gadebridge. We joined right at the outset and by the time Henry had retired in 1965 we had learned to play carpet bowls and bridge. This resulted in us having a busy social life and meeting lots of people. Our circle of friends grew. Life seemed good and we were now relishing it in our mid sixties.

Our neighbours, although much younger than us, were very friendly and were always offering to help in one way or another. It was so different from living in a large town or city where neighbours can be anonymous.

Twenty-three

It is a fact of life that you should always embrace the moment. My health had deteriorated rapidly during the past few years and by the age of seventy I was no longer able to venture far from the house and when I did I had to use a wheelchair. I was frustrated by my poor health and aware that it made me short tempered. I also became increasingly impatient with people and I had a very short fuse, as far as Henry was concerned.

During the times I was alone I used the wonderful gift that I still possessed, that of my memory. I used to close my eyes and return to many places, especially Canada. I revisited it in all the seasons. I felt the warm sunshine under the dappled shade of the trees in Victoria Park. I could see the colours of the fall flash before me then miles of virgin snow as if viewed from the train. The trees were covered in white, their branches festooned with diamonds. It all seemed so real. I could even hear the sound of the train thundering along the track. Its reassuring rhythm frequently sent me to sleep but I always awoke to the reality of my life with the pain of memories that I preferred not to re-examine.

Henry realised that with my health declining, our house presented a problem because the bathroom was upstairs. Although retirement gave him plenty of time to care for me, it meant we were in each other's company constantly, day and night. This situation brought its problems and tensions mounted. We became increasingly irritated with each other. Our pasts were revived, revisited and judged, sometimes unfairly. We were both as bad as each other. We had both gone through so much, even before we had met and married. I don't know why we were surprised by our emotional debris relentlessly resurfacing. Guilt was rooted in our souls. Henry and I were both capable of walking the path of self destruction. Perhaps a move allowing us more personal space would help? I certainly prayed that this would be so. Our days and nights continued to merge into one, with us either persistently backbiting or competing over who would be the first to break the oppressive spells of silence.

Henry confided some of our problems to a social worker. Her advice was to apply for a ground floor flat or a retirement bungalow. We took her advice and applied for a transfer. We were accepted and promised the very next suitable property available. We realised that it could take some time. During the next six months the arguing and bickering was unrelenting until we reached an impasse. In the end we managed to talk amicably, declared a truce and agreed that we would abide by our wedding vows that committed us for better or worse. Life became a little more tolerable. We tried to avoid confrontations and left the past well and truly behind. Sadly the bouts of silence between us became greater than ever before.

I watched for the post each day. Occasionally a letter would arrive from Lillian, which always pleased us but deep down in my heart, I was always watching out for one from Thomas, imagining he might write to correct all the bad things he had said and done.

Finally, a letter arrived from the housing department offering us a bungalow in Forest Walk which was close to the shops, dentist and the doctor. We were delighted and accepted by return post. Suddenly the panic set in. How on earth would we be able to move?

We had no children to help us and our circle of friends had diminished. Those who were still alive had become too old and frail to assist. Our home help May related our predicament to several people and very quickly the word spread to The Halsey, a senior school very near to where we were moving. A sixth form tutor asked for volunteers to assist with the move. Apparently, the whole form raised their hands and agreed to help.

The move went like clockwork. Some of the boys' fathers also got involved and they came and packed boxes and crates. A few mothers decided to join in too; they hung curtains and made up beds for the night. Our fridge was mysteriously filled and we never found out who the Good Samaritan was. We were entertained by a neighbour for that day and late in the afternoon we were taken to our new home, sat down and given a tray of tea. It was all so unbelievable and we both appreciated all the effort put in by the volunteers. I may even have smiled for the first time in months.

JANE

1974 - 2012

Twenty-four

I continued to make my weekly visits to Esther. Some weeks were easier than others. I still witnessed the animosity between Esther and Henry and found it hard to understand. I decided that it would be better for me in the long run if I accepted that my only function in the house was to care for the patient. It was easy to think and say but harder to follow. The only time I saw a chink in the armour that they had built around themselves was when May called in, to see if they needed any shopping. Esther used to relax and produce a smile. Henry also appeared more at ease. May's unofficial visits were always curtailed as they were never longer than it took for the three of them to smoke a cigarette.

Week after week the same routine was adhered to. If it proved a good visit, Esther produced a smile but I felt it was always false and not from the heart. I found it exasperating to work in silence so I would chat about my family or relate the current news of the day. Henry was forever looking at me as though he was weighing me up and making an assessment of some kind.

Apart from the one time when I asked about the two photographs neither Esther nor Henry mentioned anything about having children. The story behind the shawl intrigued me. I guessed something traumatic had happened which Esther didn't want to talk about. Maybe the memory of it was just too painful to contemplate. Little did she know that it wasn't just curiosity with me.

My mother-in-law knitted beautifully and made shawls and hand knits for all our children. During my second pregnancy, Mum started a new shawl which she became increasingly irritated with. Every couple of rows she worked she had to unravel as the pattern was out of line. With three hundred stitches on two needles, to unwind and re-knit this again was no mean feat. It frustrated her. I became concerned at the angst it was causing her and told her to stop. I would use my first baby's shawl. At eight months my baby was stillborn. I too had an incomplete shawl, the only difference being that my mother-in-law threw away both the knitting and the remaining wool.

In time I fell pregnant again and when my second baby daughter was born her grandmother presented her with a new shawl. Mum hadn't made a wrong stitch in its completion. It was perfect. We don't know or understand many of the mysteries of life. We have to accept the things that cannot be explained and move on.

It took quite some time before Esther enquired about my children. My son was a good basketball player and she would ask about his progress. I gathered from comments that she made that she knew quite a bit about basketball. It became obvious that she had gained that knowledge in Canada where the game was well known.

Over time I gradually became more at ease and comfortable in Esther and Henry's company. I remember very clearly a momentous day which affirmed my acceptance. Their front door had been left ajar for me. I tapped on the door and called my usual greeting of, "It's only me."

Esther looked up from her chair and called to Henry.

"Here comes the sunshine."

I was elated, not only had my ego had a boost but it showed genuine emotions from both Esther and Henry.

My own life was about to change in a surprising way. My husband had served in the Royal Navy during the Second World War and was a survivor of a bombed ship. The surviving crew were rescued and taken to Durban, South Africa. My husband and his friend were taken in by a family called the Winters who lived in Port Elizabeth. They were so kind to him and several of his fellow sailors that they formed a close friendship. Their kindness gave Bill a love of both the family and their lovely country.

Bill's mother and father had both passed away in 1969 and we felt it was the right time in our lives to fulfil our dream and emigrate to South Africa. Our eldest daughter Melanie was already married and our second daughter, Andrea was at college training to teach. Naturally Nigel, our son would accompany us, as he was only fourteen. A job was procured for Bill so we only had to wait for the immigration department to grant us permanent residency. In those days you had to prove that you were solvent and had a working contract. We were able to provide all the relevant paperwork and meet the requirements but we still had a wait of six months before we received all the documentation granting us visas.

At this stage we had only told the closest members of the family of our intentions. My first job was to hand in my notice to the nursing officer. It was quite an easy task to inform most of my patients but my biggest dread was to come. I had to tell the Taylors. With my new name of Sunshine and the fact that they loathed South Africa, I felt at a disadvantage.

I slowly walked up the path to the Taylors' home feeling the same trepidation that I experienced on my first solo visit to them four years earlier. As soon as I said my usual, "It's only me." Esther replied speedily,

"What's the matter? Your voice sounds anxious."

Esther's quick off the mark response did me a favour as all my rehearsed explanations were now unnecessary.

"I am leaving my job and we are moving."

It took a split second for Esther to burst into tears. I instinctively moved towards the armchair to comfort her but to my astonishment Henry moved forward and put his arms around her shoulders. After Esther had regained her composure I completed my routine tasks then sat with her and Henry to have a coffee. Now was as good a time as any to relate our intentions to emigrate and to state where we intended to live. It was as though a bomb had been dropped.

"Oh no," was their joint reply.

"It's such a heathen country," shrieked Esther.

Henry's inborn dislike and distrust of South Africa as a nation was overpowering and had resulted in influencing Esther. I still hadn't a clue why he hated South Africa so much. I realised that nothing positive would be achieved so I drew things to a close and stood up.

"I will see you as usual next week. It will be my last week of working for the district nursing group. Bye for now."

I left with a sinking heart, feeling nauseous and a little shaky. My eyes were brimming with tears. These emotions made me realise that you cannot mix your professional life with your personal one. I always knew this but I had broken the rules. My last visits to all my patients were a mixture of regret and hope. I knew that I wouldn't be seeing many of them again and I needed to trust that our future life would be worth the price being paid.

I had enjoyed my job and most of my patients were of an age to have both children and grandchildren. They would often tell me of the little goings-on that most families experience. That was the difference with the Taylors. There was no family background that I could talk to them about. As always, Esther's was the last house that I would visit. It was sad and I could feel their anxiety. However, it did have its lighter moments. Esther told me that she didn't want a replacement nurse. The new auxiliary nurse who was to replace me would suffer for a few weeks, I thought. History would repeat itself, no doubt.

For some reason, I glanced at the mantel shelf to see the usual small glass half filled with brandy. On my first visit I was of the opinion that the glass would have been filled many times in any given day. I was so wrong. When I had got to know Esther quite well she told me that when she was ill in Canada, she had been told by her doctor to always keep a small brandy near her and that if she felt very anxious she should sip it. I had made an assumption that was completely wide of the mark. I learned a lesson from it, to be less judgemental, as I had been on my first visit to Esther.

The time for our departure was fast approaching. Our house was sold, furniture given away and treasures packed by the shipping company. Farewells are always tough, love comes with a price.

Bill came with me to say goodbye to the Taylors. He had met them several times. He used to drop me off, and then collect me, whenever he needed the car. I appreciated Bill accompanying me for support. I was surprised that the Taylors were quite controlled and wished us well, extracting a promise that I would write as soon as we were settled. I was glad to give them that assurance.

Our flight was without incident until we were approaching Johannesburg. The pilot made an announcement over the tannoy.

"Will the family Durrant please raise their hands."

The captain informed all the passengers on the flight that we were immigrants starting a new life in South Africa. He then asked them to show that we were most welcome. Everybody clapped. I just dissolved into tears. My brother had arranged the welcome with the South African Airways pilot.

Life became a hectic round of house hunting, buying furniture, appliances and so on. My son started school and hated it. Fourteen was a difficult age to start a new school and to transfer to a different system of exams etc. However, his skills in basketball gave him one big advantage as it was a new game in South African schools. Nigel was up to county standard at home. The school appreciated his talent and excused him from the compulsory learning of Afrikaans. That was the only plus as far as he was concerned. Bill found it difficult to settle into his job. The weekly board room meetings were quite a strain on him as he was unused to such procedures. As for me, I was mentally drained trying to support the men in my life. I thought the most important word for us all to absorb was 'adapt.'

We bought and moved into a very pleasant house in a suburb of Durban called Pinetown. It was only a twenty minute drive to the city centre. The house was built on one level, what we'd call a bungalow in the UK. It was incredibly spacious with a very large overgrown garden. We found out that the previous owners had been landscape gardeners but the house had been left unattended for quite a time and the weeds were trying to regain control. With a team of garden lads and me as their supervisor, we restored the grounds to their original glory. It was exciting to steadily reveal the exquisite plants uncovered in each flower bed.

Lawns sloped down to the road behind the house and all the garden was enclosed by a ten foot high poinsettia hedge. When the red bracts were at their best it looked magnificent. Adjacent to this glory was an orchard which was separated from the lawn area by high cherry tree hedging. Every day brought new pleasures. We found lemons, grapes both black and white on the same vines. The previous owners had grafted one variety onto the rootstock of another. A bed of pineapples lay at their feet. It was all such a marvel to us, as each day something new was discovered in the grounds.

We had been warned to look out for snakes but during all the extensive work we only found one shed skin, probably that of a brown house snake. These snakes are completely harmless and are good to have as they keep the wild rodent population levels down to a minimum around the home. Brightly coloured purple crested turacos lived in the avocado tree and were truly magnificent. I had never seen birds like these outside an aviary. I couldn't believe they were in our garden. Unfortunately, their stay was short lived for as soon as we got Ringo and Tara, two rescue dogs, they took flight never to return.

My time was taken up supervising the garden lads, doing the school run and picking Bill up from work. Our day started early. Bill and Nigel both set off for work and school at seven a.m. and finished at three in the afternoon. It gave me plenty to do at the beginning. Before long Nigel caught a school bus and Bill was given a lift to work by a colleague, which freed up my day.

On Sunday mornings I would sit and write letters home to my family and friends. I found that if we drove to Durban before four in the afternoon, my letters would catch the evening flight at 6 p.m. My mail would be received and delivered in England by the Tuesday. It became a habit for me and Bill always complied with our Sunday afternoon run to the main post office. In fact, on one occasion I had an answer from my daughter within the week, which was really amazing.

I wrote to Esther and Henry and to my delight they replied quite quickly. I was also thrilled that I still had a little corner in their hearts for Esther addressed the letter to, '*My Dear Sunshine*.' I was able to describe my life to them and I hoped that it would revise their opinion of this beautiful country. We try in life to influence people but we are not always successful. In a few cases, I think we do have an effect but the results are not always apparent. I felt that the Taylors and I had formed a relationship and bonded, if only just a little.

Life was idyllic, barbecues or braais as they are called in South Africa seemed to be given each weekend by friends or family. It was all very impressive. Having gardeners and maids meant nothing more to me than an embarrassment. I missed my previous simple life and the love of my daughters.

I lost weight and Bill was aware that I had lost my sparkle. He told me that my sadness was reflected in my eyes. After long discussions and a lot of soul searching, a decision was made to return to England. We had lived in South Africa for just over a year. It proved comforting to pack again for our return. This time we had packers to crate everything. We knew our spending would have to be kept to the minimum. Every spare penny had to be saved to buy a house and keep us, until Bill and I found jobs. All three of us were ecstatic at the thought of returning home. So many of our friends in Durban thought we would regret our return. To this day, I can honestly say, we didn't. The hardest thing for us was re-homing Ringo and Tara as they had become loyal companions. We left knowing they had both gone to good homes.

When we returned to the UK we managed to buy a moderate house and altered it to our liking. It was wonderful and heartening to see the family again. Our little grandson was a joy to us and we resumed family life as though it hadn't been interrupted. Bill returned to his old company, a friend offered me a position in the local doctors' surgery and Nigel resumed school. Living in Hemel Hempstead was the same as it was before we left but we paid a high price. The experience had had great financial implications. We lost a lot of money and Bill much of his pension rights. Even so, we both agreed that returning to England had been the right decision for us.

I enjoyed my new job. It entailed shift work which I had never done before. It fitted in well with the family commitments I had. During the year away, my mother's health declined. As soon as we were back home, daily visits to her became the norm. It was amazing that for the whole year I was in Durban my mother managed with the help of her very good friend Grace but as soon as I was back on the scene this was no longer the case and my attention was required. According to my mother, once you are eighty all mobility and reason deserts you, requiring your family to give you their undivided attention.

Esther and Henry were delighted by our return. I realised that we took the place of any children that they might have had. I would drop in to see them any time that I was in the area and on seeing me their faces would light up. It was hard to remember their dour countenances of the past.

I wish I could say that their personal relationship was closer but it wasn't so. The eternal battle for my attention prevailed. It was such a waste of the precious time that they had left. All I could do was to show them that I cared about both of them.

Their needs were small as were their appetites. The food on their plates was the amount that one would give to a small child. Henry was like a tall skeleton, Esther was slight. I hadn't seen her stand for a few years. She seemed a permanent fixture glued to the settee, like the brandy glass on the mantelpiece, which I presumed Henry would have refilled for Esther every few days.

I had forgotten how their smoking permeated everything surrounding them. Both the ceiling and the walls were nicotine yellow. I realised that any comment passed by me wouldn't be appreciated. In truth, did it matter? It was the only pleasure they shared. Very often Esther would attempt to talk to me but only when Henry had left the room. She was never able to complete what she wanted to say. I felt anxious that it could be serious. I earnestly enquired, "Esther is your health worrying you? Are you experiencing any pain?"

"No," was said with such emphasis.

I assumed it had to be something personal, that couldn't be told in five minutes so I invited them to lunch or if they preferred afternoon tea or morning coffee. Their answer always came in the form of a refusal. Henry's frequent visits to the bathroom, no doubt, influenced their reply. They were both now in their late seventies. You can only go so far without invading people's privacy. I had to back off but at the same time, be there if they felt they needed me.

My visits continued as before, the pattern never varied. I found myself racking my brains for subjects to discuss with them. I used to look at Esther's face and wonder what she was holding back from me and why. I found it odd, considering on several occasions Esther had said I was the daughter they should have had. Whatever it was, it was truly locked away. I suspected forever.

A remark one day opened a door on my past and not Esther's. She asked me about my childhood.

"Did you have a happy one?" I answered in truth and said, "Sometimes." My recall was from the age of five.

"I remember my first day at school quite clearly. We all sat in rows with the teacher holding up pictures of cats, dogs and cows to ascertain if we knew the sounds the animals made. I remember thinking that the teacher was silly because everyone knew what sounds the animals made. I also remember in the school hall there were rows of little beds and we had to have an afternoon nap. We were covered with blankets by the teacher which made me feel cosy and secure."

Esther appeared to be listening and interested and I hoped that she would interact with me and divulge something about her childhood. It wasn't to be, she just abruptly changed the subject.

On each visit I observed quite a change in both Esther and Henry. They were rapidly becoming frailer. I informed their doctor's surgery about my concerns and a home visit was scheduled. Henry was also getting a little unstable when he moved from the chair. In addition, I noticed that I was no longer offered a coffee. All signs of deterioration.

Winter was approaching. I deliberated whether I should contact social services to inform them of the Taylor's plight. I went ahead and telephoned the relevant department. I was informed that they appreciated help was needed but that they couldn't intervene on my request alone. If I was able to suggest to Esther and Henry that they themselves ask for extra help they would be happy to assist. It was a battle that I couldn't win.

May continued to call regularly and did their shopping for them at the local shops in Gadebridge. Their biggest need was for cigarettes and dog food for Tessa. To them they were the essentials.

It was Sunday and as usual I was dashing to prepare the roast lunch before going to church. Bill usually answered any telephone calls but on this occasion he was trying to finish cleaning the car in readiness for me. I took the call. The voice at the end of the telephone sounded odd, it was Henry.

"Jane I cannot wake Esther up."

My heart lurched, I replied, "Go and sit down in your chair Henry. I will be with you in a few minutes." My next task was to inform the surgery.

I arrived at the Taylor's house at the same time as the doctor and we entered the house together. The doctor stopped to talk to Henry and I went ahead to the bedroom.

I looked down at Esther. I couldn't believe my eyes. She was lying on her side with her hand on her chin. She looked so beautiful and had a slight smile. By her side on the bedside cabinet was an untouched mug of Ovaltine. She must have just put her head on the pillow and slipped away. I felt so emotional but was uplifted by the way she had died. Looking down on this serene face I knew why two men had fallen in love with her. Something painful in her life had brought about a change. It saddened me that I hadn't been able to help her.

Doctor Evans walked into the bedroom to examine

Esther and said, "She had such a peaceful death."

He signed the death certificate stating she had died from her long standing heart condition.

When the doctor left, Henry's eyes looked frightened and he appeared bewildered.

"Jane, please will you help me? I don't know what to do."

They were the first words he had uttered to me since my arrival. I was astounded that they hadn't discussed their funerals or made any arrangements concerning their deaths. I thought that with no children it would have been more important for them to have done so, than for most people who had families to support them. Both Esther and Henry had had jobs which required organisational skills which allowed me to think that they wouldn't need help when their final journeys were made. However, it wasn't a problem for me. A couple of telephone calls later I was able to reassure Henry that I was available to accompany him the next day and help with the arrangements. I arrived home feeling emotionally drained. My greatest concern was for Henry and how he would manage his future.

I arrived at Henry's home quite early the next morning. I was very apprehensive about his acceptance of Esther's death and how he would come to terms with it. I have found that however close to death people are, one always gets a shock at their demise. Henry finding Esther must have given him a terrible jolt. He then had to sleep in the same bedroom, which he must have found very emotional. Fortunately, Esther's body was removed by the undertakers as soon as the doctor had left. Henry, bless him, realised that it was also hard for me and he came over and gave me a big hug and a smile to match. I realised that he was probably experiencing a big adrenaline surge.

One of my first tasks was to telephone the dog rescue society, the one from where Tessa originated, to ask if they could board her for a couple of weeks whilst we were arranging the funeral and all the other things which needed to be done. In my heart I knew Henry would have difficulty in caring for her. Tessa hadn't been walked for a very long time. The society was very understanding and sent someone to collect her within a couple of hours.

Our next job was to register the death at Dacorum Register Office and from there drive to the Funeral Director's to make the arrangements. It was only three weeks to Christmas and a dire time to organise a funeral. We were fortunate in that it was to be a fairly low key funeral with only four of us attending. The Funeral Director was able to co-ordinate a slot for us the following week. It proved to be a very simple service but carried out with dignity. We returned to the house afterwards to a small amount of refreshments with tea, coffee or sherry. It was what Henry wanted and he remarked that it was a fitting end to Esther's life. I was not sure what he meant by that but it didn't matter.

The arrangements were completed the next day with a visit to the solicitor's and the payment of all the outstanding bills. I had been concerned about whether Henry could cover the cost of the funeral. I needn't have worried, he had sufficient funds. I had no knowledge of the Taylor's finances. I assumed that their work pensions supplemented those of the state. Esther and Henry's home didn't give me any clues. It was very stark and there was no apparent evidence of the luxuries of life such as fine china or silver. There were no family heirlooms. Towels were much worn as was the bed linen. It was very puzzling. All the bills which arrived after the funeral were settled immediately which ended my concerns.

Life for Henry resumed but not with the same routine as before. Tessa was re-homed with one of the dog walkers who already knew her. Although this was a wrench for Henry he knew it was the best thing for Tessa. We were both pleased with that outcome.

Henry's health greatly concerned me. I could see he was fading away before my eyes. Christmas was now only a few days away. I invited Henry to our home but he declined as he was embarrassed by his frequent use of the bathroom. I called to see him on Christmas Eve taking some suitable food for him to eat the following day. It was food that he could manage to deal with. I felt uneasy about leaving him alone. Next morning I prepared our Christmas lunch and left it all, complete with guests, in the capable hands of my husband. I knew he would watch over everything and I felt I needed to pop in on Henry.

When I arrived at Henry's home I let myself in. Henry had entrusted me with a key. I found Henry looking so ill, lying across his bed unable to climb inside the sheets. After telephoning the on duty doctor I managed to disrobe Henry and find some clean pyjamas for him. It was such a struggle as he was unable to help me. My silent prayers were answered and I found the strength.

It was only when I went to get some clean linen that I discovered all the sheets had already been used and needed washing. As I opened the airing cupboard door the stench of urine physically knocked me backwards and I had to use all my self control to prevent myself from being sick. I can still bring to mind the smell today. My heart went out to Henry. He must have been so stressed at being in such a predicament.

The arrival of the doctor proved of no help whatsoever, as there wasn't a hospital bed to be had until the New Year. I didn't return home for five days. Bill drove to the bungalow and brought me my toiletries, clean clothes and my dressing gown.

The bedroom was quite dark and very depressing. An odour of decay filled the small oppressive space. Stale cigarettes, urine and the hum of Tessa still lingered. I wanted to rise above the fog of smells. I felt the weight of Henry's sorrow. I looked down at Henry knowing that these precious moments could be his last. I was sitting on his bed with my back to the headboard and Henry's head was cradled in my lap. I felt like a mother comforting a child. It was a very tender, almost spiritual experience.

Henry asked me to tell him tales of my childhood and other stories of my life, including recent ones. Whenever

I stopped in between the tales to rest or compose myself he said, "Don't stop. Tell me some more."

I ran out of my assortment of sagas and then Henry started to relate events from his own life and Esther's. I was mesmerised by them all. I felt as though I was in the auditorium of a theatre watching one amazing play after another. I was transfixed.

I still feel privileged that he wanted to share their lives with me, both the good and the bad. He began with his early life from the first days of his recall. It was remarkable. I felt I was travelling with him on his life's journey, sharing his experiences of school, the army, and his marriages. He revealed everything to me even a particular surprising event that happened in the winter of 1964.

On that evening as Esther and Henry were sitting down relaxing, watching television, a knock resounded from the front door. Henry got up from his armchair and opened the door to find a tall woman standing on the doorstep. She seemed very anxious. Henry asked how he could help her. She answered by saying that she was related to Sarah, Henry's former wife. Henry knew instantly that this had to be true and asked her to wait. He politely shut the door in order to inform Esther.

Esther agreed that the woman had to have some connection to them and told Henry to invite her in. She was invited into the sitting room, asked to sit down and was offered a cup of tea.

Henry asked, "Would you like to take your coat off?

Now, what can we do for you?"

The woman declined both and perched hesitantly on the edge of the small sofa in her turquoise coat and toning sling back shoes. Next came the bombshell. The timid woman looked up at Henry from under her black fringe.

"I am Samuel, your son."

Henry and Esther were stunned. They were in a state of shock, horror and disbelief. Eventually Samuel's voice broke through the ringing silence.

"Can I have that cup of tea now?"

Samuel sipped at his tea and related his story. He told Esther and Henry that he had known he was a transsexual from an early age. He had never felt comfortable as a boy and had always felt he was inside the wrong body. When he had plucked up enough courage to tell his mother she was horrified. His confession led to him being made to leave home.

Sarah had refused to accept the fact and made Samuel promise not to tell his father as she felt it would reflect badly on him as a serving soldier. Plus he would be more than shocked to have a son who, as she put it, was sometimes a woman. At this point Samuel dissolved into tears and became very distressed. This triggered painful memories for Henry who then broke down himself. It was all too much for Esther. Before too long, all three of them were sobbing, connected by their grief.

Samuel went on to say why he had decided to trace his father. He was desperate and urgently needed money to fund his final sex reassignment surgery.

Henry continued with the story and told me how he had shouted at Sam, which was now his son's preferred name, and then how Esther had joined in too telling him to get out of the house and that they would never give him any money.

Henry said that he thought the woman he had opened the door to was somewhat masculine from the start even though she had a tender, feminine voice. There was something about her height and broad shoulders, her whole body was broad. Esther felt that Sam would have passed for a woman anywhere. He finished relating the story by saying, "Jane, if it was now, I would have listened to him but it still disgusts me." What a sorry tale. I found tears were pouring down my face at the sadness of it all. From that day, nothing more was heard of from Sam.

Henry's talks progressed to stories of Esther's past. I was intrigued by her childhood and the fact that she was one of the country's first WRAFs. I always felt that there was much more to Esther than the embittered lady that I had got to know.

It still amazes me that Henry's last six days revealed so much about his past. When looking at Henry towards the end it was hard to imagine that he once stood over six feet six inches tall and would have looked resplendent in his Life Guard's uniform. He was a dignified gentleman, in every sense of the word. Once respected by his peers but now lying in bed, he looked especially vulnerable. Although he was extremely weak and frail he managed to summon the strength to relate so much of his past. It was as though he needed to unburden his soul.

Twenty-five

Henry was getting frailer by the hour. Frantic calls to the appropriate authorities were made by me every few hours. I knew what the trouble was. Henry just needed care and not a diagnosis. Beds were not available to him. Henry was finally admitted to hospital on 29th December. I locked the house and decided to tidy up on my return from Wales. Bill and I were spending the New Year with my sister and her family. Henry died on 1st January 1979. I returned that very day but too late to say goodbye to him. I was upset but not surprised and had to be grateful that Henry's demise wasn't prolonged. It was now time to organise Henry's funeral. His solicitor was the other executor. He left me to arrange everything as I had done for Esther.

The funeral took place on a wet, cold miserable day which carried with it the depression that post Christmas can sometimes bring. This time it was even more noticeable that the mourners were few, just May, Bill and myself.

My next visit to the solicitor was to discuss the content of Henry's Last Will and Testament. I also needed to know if all the expenses could be funded once again. The bills were met from the estate.

Henry carried out the wishes of both Esther and himself by leaving all their money to a home for deaf children based in Marble Arch. They left £1,223 to the charity and £100 to me. The solicitor subsequently found that the school had been closed and the building demolished. The money was donated to the Royal National Institute for the Blind, for the specific use of the Sunshine Fund for children. I was informed that my legacy had been added by Henry after Esther's death. Apparently, he gave the solicitor instructions in writing.

As I was about to leave the solicitor's office he said,

"We have to make an appointment to meet at the Taylor's home to sort out the contents."

"Yes, of course. You'll need to wear your old clothes and bring some rubber gloves. We must also make arrangements with the council as they will need to take everything to the tip."

He immediately amended his comments. "On second thoughts, I don't think I will bother. You appear very capable. I will leave it all to you to deal with."

I make no further comment on his parting remarks.

Between Esther dying and Henry becoming very ill I had paid a bill on behalf of Henry to a television rental company. It was an advance payment to cover the six months ahead. With permission from the solicitor I retrieved the money and bought a piece of jewellery for May. I couldn't believe that she hadn't been remembered by Esther or Henry in their wills. For years she had looked after them, getting shopping and their prescriptions from the surgery. She was so touched that they had remembered her. I am sure that had Esther and Henry given thought to their wills, they would have made a provision for May.

My next task was to contact Lillian. Both Molly and Jim had died and I had no knowledge of the whereabouts of their children. I wrote to Lillian informing her of her in-laws deaths. She promptly replied and we kept up a correspondence. Although not on a regular basis, it was for several years. After a period of receiving no answers from her I became concerned and wrote several letters to the resident at her address requesting information. My letters were never answered. I had to let things go and realised that this was the second unresolved mystery in Canada.

Now the heartache really started. I had learned so much from Henry's stories that the sentiment I felt was that of a daughter clearing out the parental home. I let myself into the bungalow a little earlier than I had arranged with May. It took such an effort to enter the bedroom as the last time I was there I left behind a room full of sorrow, regret and strangely, love. Sitting on Esther's bed, looking at Henry's, caused memories to come flooding back. Esther's and Henry's tormented lives had taught me a lot about myself. Tears soon trickled down my cheeks. Where had all their love gone? I felt the pain of silence.

May's ringing of the doorbell brought me sharply back to the task in hand. She walked through the hallway bright and breezy.

"Morning Jane. How are you? Don't be sad.Their passing was a blessing and a happy release. They are both at rest now."

I wasn't so sure.

May returned to the bungalow several times during the following week to help me. There were no hidden treasures. I couldn’t begin to imagine where their precious possessions or money had gone. We found nothing, only a little spare change in one of Henry’s pockets and a couple of pounds in a wallet. It was all so heart-rending.

I decided to bin the contents of the airing cupboard. I felt disloyal putting the bed linen into black plastic bags for disposal. My instinct was to take the linen home and return it freshly laundered and ironed. Out came the threadbare towels and various curtains, faded and yellow with smoke and time. I also removed some very discoloured plastic carrier bags which contained postcards from the First World War plus more from the intervening years. In another bag were numerous letters, a few medals and a square of purple silk with battle names printed upon it. I carefully placed everything in one of the larger plastic carrier bags I had found with several more letters and various paper documents. The entire collection of letters, cards, photos and papers was in disarray and very grubby. I recall looking down at my hands to see that they were black from years of grime.

The local authority turned up as scheduled to remove the entire contents of the home. I don't know why but I saved the carrier bag from the council's truck. I didn't have an interest in the letters or feel intrigued by the contents. As the workmen were placing the old worn furniture on the lorry I glimpsed an old cigar box. It was full of bits and bobs too filthy to distinguish what was what. However, the box and its contents ended up in the plastic bag as well.

I looked at the men carrying the final boxes away from the Taylor's home and my sadness descended once more. Is this all you are worth after a lifetime of giving and loving? I questioned my own future and hoped that I would never end up in the same situation without a grieving family and friends. We all think that it will not happen to us. I am in no doubt that Esther and Henry would have said the same. I washed my hands, locked the door and walked away with my bulging carrier bag.

May nor I thought to look in the loft or garden shed. It is only now with hind sight on writing the Taylor's story that I realise Henry would never have parted with his beloved violin let alone his clarinet or army memorabilia.

Twenty-six

On my arrival home Bill ran a hot bath for me. I closed the door, lowered myself into the therapeutic soothing water and cried and cried. I was feeling the loss of family. I was astounded at how involved I had become. I had made Esther and Henry part of my family. A knock on the door from Bill offering me a comforting cup of tea brought me back to the reality of my own family and I vowed to learn a lesson from this - never involve myself again. But of course I did and still do.

Life returned to my usual daily routine of going to work and keeping my focus on my mother's declining mobility. The Taylor's carrier bag had been left in my small bedroom where I did my ironing. Whilst ironing I could smell a musty odour emanating from the bag and felt I had to do one of two things, either investigate the contents or dispose of it.

Over the next few weeks I picked odd letters out and started to read them. Most were dated and I was able to organise them chronologically. There were letters from

Esther's father sent to her in Canada after the First World War. So many letters gave me information about Esther's background. There were papers with reference to Henry's life from birth to adulthood - birth, marriage and death certificates. I now knew so much about their lives. I discovered the truth about Henry's father's tragic death and I found his war medals.

The contents proved to be awesome in their revelations. An almost completed picture at long last. I now knew more about their lives than they did of each others, they had kept so much from one another. Now I was the guardian of their secrets having been captivated and more or less absorbed in to their amazing life stories.

I hearkened back to the day of the council's workmen removing the contents of the Taylor's home and my feeling of, was this all? It certainly wasn't. I didn't walk out of their house with a bag of rubbish. I was carrying riches that were and still are to this day beyond any price.

Lightning Source UK Ltd.
Milton Keynes UK
UKOW04f0054181213

223210UK00001B/1/P

9 781784 072124

